THE MODERN LIBRARY
OF THE WORLD'S BEST BOOKS

MEN, WOMEN AND BOATS

TURN TO THE END OF THIS VOLUME FOR A COMPLETE LIST OF TITLES IN THE MODERN LIBRARY.

MEN, WOMEN AND BOATS

BY STEPHEN CRANE

EDITED WITH AN INTRODUCTION BY
VINCENT STARRETT

BONI AND LIVERIGHT

PUBLISHERS ⋰ ⋱ NEW YORK

MEN, WOMEN AND BOATS

NOTE

A NUMBER of the tales and sketches here brought together appear now for the first time between covers; others for the first time between covers in this country. All have been gathered from out-of-print volumes and old magazine files.

"The Open Boat," one of Stephen Crane's finest stories, is used with the courteous permission of Doubleday, Page & Co., holders of the copyright. Its companion masterpiece, "The Blue Hotel," because of copyright complications, has had to be omitted, greatly to the regret of the editor.

After the death of Stephen Crane, a haphazard and un-discriminating gathering of his earlier tales and sketches appeared in London under the misleading title, "Last Words." From this volume, now rarely met with, a number of characteristic minor works have been selected, and these will be new to Crane's American admirers; as follows: "The Reluctant Voyagers," "The End of the Battle," "The Upturned Face," "An Episode of War," "A Desertion," "Four Men in a Cave," "The Mesmeric Mountain," "London Impressions," "The Snake."

Three of our present collection, printed by arrangement, appeared in the London (1898) edition of "The Open Boat and Other Stories," published by William Heinemann, but did not occur in the American volume of that title. They are "An Experiment in Misery," "The Duel that was not Fought," and "The Pace of Youth."

For the rest, "A Dark Brown Dog," "A Tent in Agony," and "The Scotch Express," are here printed for the first time in a book.

For the general title of the present collection, the editor alone is responsible.

V. S.

MEN, WOMEN AND BOATS

CONTENTS

STEPHEN CRANE: *AN ESTIMATE*

STEPHEN CRANE: AN ESTIMATE

IT hardly profits us to conjecture what Stephen Crane might have written about the World War had he lived.   Certainly, he would have been in it, in one capacity or another. No man had a greater talent for war and personal adventure, nor a finer art in describing it.   Few writers of recent times could so well describe the poetry of motion as manifested in the surge and flow of battle, or so well depict the isolated deed of heroism in its stark simplicity and terror.

To such an undertaking as Henri Barbusse's "Under Fire," that powerful, brutal book, Crane would have brought an analytical genius almost clairvoyant.   He possessed an uncanny vision; a descriptive ability photographic in its clarity and its care for minutiæ—yet unphotographic in that the big central thing often is omitted, to be felt rather than seen in the occult suggestion of detail.   Crane would have seen and depicted the grisly horror of it all, as did Barbusse, but also he would have seen the glory and the ecstasy and the wonder of it, and over that his poetry would have been spread.

While Stephen Crane was an excellent psychologist, he was also a true poet.   Frequently his prose was finer poetry than his deliberate essays in poesy.   His most famous book, "The Red Badge of Courage," is essentially a psychological study, a delicate clinical dissection of the soul of a recruit, but it is also a *tour de force* of the imagination.   When he wrote the book he had never seen a battle: he had to place himself in the situation of another. Years later, when he came out of the Greco-Turkish *fracas*, he remarked to a friend: " 'The Red Badge' is all right."

Written by a youth who had scarcely passed his majority, this book has been compared with Tolstoy's "Sebastopol" and Zola's "La Débâcle," and with some of the short stories of Ambrose Bierce. The comparison with Bierce's work is legitimate; with the other books, I think, less so. Tolstoy and Zola see none of the traditional beauty of battle; they apply themselves to a devoted—almost obscene—study of corpses and carnage generally; and they lack the American's instinct for the rowdy commonplace, the natural, the irreverent, which so materially aids his realism. In "The Red Badge of Courage" invariably the tone is kept down where one expects a height: the most heroic deeds are accomplished with studied awkwardness.

Crane was an obscure free-lance when he wrote this book. The effort, he says, somewhere, "was born of pain—despair, almost." It was a better piece of work, however, for that very reason, as Crane knew. It is far from flawless. It has been remarked that it bristles with as many grammatical errors as with bayonets; but it is a big canvas, and I am certain that many of Crane's deviations from the rules of polite rhetoric were deliberate experiments, looking to effect—effect which, frequently, he gained.

Stephen Crane "arrived" with this book. There are, of course, many who never have heard of him, to this day, but there was a time when he was very much talked of. That was in the middle nineties, following publication of "The Red Badge of Courage," although even before that he had occa-

sioned a brief flurry with his weird collection of poems called
"The Black Riders and Other Lines." He was highly praised,
and highly abused and laughed at; but he seemed to be
"made." We have largely forgotten since. It is a way we
have.

Personally, I prefer his short stories to his novels and his
poems; those, for instance, contained in "The Open Boat,"
in "Wounds in the Rain," and in "The Monster." The title-
story in that first collection is perhaps his finest piece of work.
Yet what is it? A truthful record of an adventure of his
own in the filibustering days that preceded our war with
Spain; the faithful narrative of the voyage of an open boat,
manned by a handful of shipwrecked men. But Captain
Bligh's account of *his* small boat journey, after he had been
sent adrift by the mutineers of the *Bounty,* seems tame in
comparison, although of the two the English sailor's voyage
was the more perilous.

In "The Open Boat" Crane again gains his effects by keeping down the tone where another writer might have attempted
"fine writing" and have been lost. In it perhaps is most
strikingly evident the poetic cadences of his prose: its rhyth-
mic, monotonous flow is the flow of the gray water that laps
at the sides of the boat, that rises and recedes in cruel waves,
"like little pointed rocks." It is a desolate picture, and the
tale is one of our greatest short stories. In the other tales
that go to make up the volume are wild, exotic glimpses of
Latin-America. I doubt whether the color and spirit of that
region have been better rendered than in Stephen Crane's
curious, distorted, staccato sentences.

"War Stories" is the laconic sub-title of "Wounds in the

Rain." It was not war on a grand scale that Crane saw in the Spanish-American complication, in which he participated as a war correspondent; no such war as the recent horror. But the occasions for personal heroism were no fewer than always, and the opportunities for the exercise of such powers of trained and appreciative understanding and sympathy as Crane possessed, were abundant. For the most part, these tales are episodic, reports of isolated instances—the profanely humorous experiences of correspondents, the magnificent courage of signalmen under fire, the forgotten adventure of a converted yacht—but all are instinct with the red fever of war, and are backgrounded with the choking smoke of battle. Never again did Crane attempt the large canvas of "The Red Badge of Courage." Before he had seen war, he imagined its immensity and painted it with the fury and fidelity of a Verestchagin; when he was its familiar, he singled out its minor, crimson passages for briefer but no less careful delineation.

In this book, again, his sense of the poetry of motion is vividly evident. We see men going into action, wave on wave, or in scattering charges; we hear the clink of their accoutrements and their breath whistling through their teeth. They are not men going into action at all, but men going about their business, which at the moment happens to be the capture of a trench. They are neither heroes nor cowards. Their faces reflect no particular emotion save, perhaps, a desire to get somewhere. They are a line of men running for a train, or following a fire engine, or charging a trench. It is a relentless picture, ever changing, ever the same. But it contains poetry, too, in rich, memorable passages.

In "The Monster and Other Stories," there is a tale called "The Blue Hotel." A Swede, its central figure, toward the end manages to get himself murdered. Crane's description of it is just as casual as that. The story fills a dozen pages of the book; but the social injustice of the whole world is hinted in that space; the upside-downness of creation, right prostrate, wrong triumphant,—a mad, crazy world. The incident of the murdered Swede is just part of the backwash of it all, but it is an illuminating fragment. The Swede was slain, not by the gambler whose knife pierced his thick hide: he was the victim of a condition for which he was no more to blame than the man who stabbed him. Stephen Crane thus speaks through the lips of one of the characters:—

> "We are all in it! This poor gambler isn't even a noun. He is a kind of an adverb. Every sin is the result of a collaboration. We, five of us, have collaborated in the murder of this Swede. Usually there are from a dozen to forty women really involved in every murder, but in this case it seems to be only five men—you, I, Johnnie, old Scully, and that fool of an unfortunate gambler came merely as a culmination, the apex of a human movement, and gets all the punishment."

And then this typical and arresting piece of irony:—

> "The corpse of the Swede, alone in the saloon, had its eyes fixed upon a dreadful legend that dwelt atop of the cash-machine: 'This registers the amount of your purchase.'"

In "The Monster," the ignorance, prejudice and cruelty of

an entire community are sharply focussed. The realism is painful; one blushes for mankind. But while this story really belongs in the volume called "Whilomville Stories," it is properly left out of that series. The Whilomville stories are pure comedy, and "The Monster" is a hideous tragedy.

Whilomville is any obscure little village one may happen to think of. To write of it with such sympathy and understanding, Crane must have done some remarkable listening in Boyville. The truth is, of course, he was a boy himself— "a wonderful boy," somebody called him—and was possessed of the boy mind. These tales are chiefly funny because they are so true—boy stories written for adults; a child, I suppose, would find them dull. In none of his tales is his curious understanding of human moods and emotions better shown.

A stupid critic once pointed out that Crane, in his search for striking effects, had been led into "frequent neglect of the time-hallowed rights of certain words," and that in his pursuit of color he "falls occasionally into almost ludicrous mishap." The smug pedantry of the quoted lines is sufficient answer to the charges, but in support of these assertions the critic quoted certain passages and phrases. He objected to cheeks "scarred" by tears, to "dauntless" statues, and to "terror-stricken" wagons. The very touches of poetic impressionism that largely make for Crane's greatness, are cited to prove him an ignoramus. There is the finest of poetic imagery in the suggestions subtly conveyed by Crane's tricky adjectives, the use of which was as deliberate with him as his choice of a subject. But Crane was an imagist before our modern imagists were known.

This unconventional use of adjectives is marked in the

Whilomville tales. In one of them Crane refers to the "solemn odor of burning turnips." It is the most nearly perfect characterization of burning turnips conceivable: can anyone improve upon that "solemn odor"?

Stephen Crane's first venture was "Maggie: A Girl of the Streets." It was, I believe, the first hint of naturalism in American letters. It was not a best-seller; it offers no solution of life; it is an episodic bit of slum fiction, ending with the tragic finality of a Greek drama. It is a skeleton of a novel rather than a novel, but it is a powerful outline, written about a life Crane had learned to know as a newspaper reporter in New York. It is a singularly fine piece of analysis, or a bit of extraordinarily faithful reporting, as one may prefer; but not a few French and Russian writers have failed to accomplish in two volumes what Crane achieved in two hundred pages. In the same category is "George's Mother," a triumph of inconsequential detail piling up with a cumulative effect quite overwhelming.

Crane published two volumes of poetry — "The Black Riders" and "War is Kind." Their appearance in print was jeeringly hailed; yet Crane was only pioneering in the free verse that is to-day, if not definitely accepted, at least more than tolerated. I like the following love poem as well as any rhymed and conventionally metrical ballad that I know:—

> "Should the wide world roll away,
>   Leaving black terror,
>   Limitless night,
>   Nor God, nor man, nor place to stand
>   Would be to me essential,
>   If thou and thy white arms were there
>   And the fall to doom a long way."

"If war be kind," wrote a clever reviewer, when the second volume appeared, "then Crane's verse may be poetry, Beardsley's black and white creations may be art, and this may be called a book";—a smart summing up that is cherished by cataloguers to this day, in describing the volume for collectors. Beardsley needs no defenders, and it is fairly certain that the clever reviewer had not read the book, for certainly Crane had no illusions about the kindness of war. The title-poem of the volume is an amazingly beautiful satire which answers all criticism.

> "Do not weep, maiden, for war is kind.
>   Because your lover threw wild hands toward the sky
>   And the affrighted steed ran on alone,
>   Do not weep.
>   War is kind.
>
> "Hoarse, booming drums of the regiment,
>   Little souls who thirst for fight,
>   These men were born to drill and die.
>   The unexplained glory flies above them,
>   Great is the battle-god, and his kingdom—
>   A field where a thousand corpses lie.
>   * * * * * *
> "Mother whose heart hung humble as a button
>   On the bright splendid shroud of your son,
>   Do not weep.
>   War is kind."

Poor Stephen Crane! Like most geniuses, he had his weaknesses and his failings; like many, if not most, geniuses, he was ill. He died of tuberculosis, tragically young. But what a comrade he must have been, with his extraordinary vision, his keen, sardonic comment, his fearlessness and his failings!

Just a glimpse of Crane's last days is afforded by a letter

written from England by Robert Barr, his friend—Robert Barr, who collaborated with Crane in "The O' Ruddy," a rollicking tale of old Ireland, or, rather, who completed it at Crane's death, to satisfy his friend's earnest request. The letter is dated from Hillhead, Woldingham, Surrey, June 8, 1900, and runs as follows:—

"My Dear——

"I was delighted to hear from you, and was much interested to see the article on Stephen Crane you sent me. It seems to me the harsh judgment of an unappreciative, commonplace person on a man of genius. Stephen had many qualities which lent themselves to misapprehension, but at the core he was the finest of men, generous to a fault, with something of the old-time recklessness which used to gather in the ancient literary taverns of London. I always fancied that Edgar Allan Poe revisited the earth as Stephen Crane, trying again, succeeding again, failing again, and dying ten years sooner than he did on the other occasion of his stay on earth.

"When your letter came I had just returned from Dover, where I stayed four days to see Crane off for the Black Forest. There was a thin thread of hope that he might recover, but to me he looked like a man already dead. When he spoke, or, rather, whispered, there was all the accustomed humor in his sayings. I said to him that I would go over to the Schwarzwald in a few weeks, when he was getting better, and that we would take some convalescent rambles together. As his wife was listening he said faintly: 'I'll look forward to that,' but he smiled at me, and winked slowly, as much as to say: 'You damned humbug, you know I'll take no more rambles in this world.' Then, as if the train of thought suggested what was looked on before as the crisis of his illness, he murmured: 'Robert, when you come to the hedge—that we must all go over— it isn't bad. You feel sleepy—and—you don't care. Just a little dreamy curiosity—which world you're really in—that's all.'

"To-morrow, Saturday, the 9th, I go again to Dover to meet his body. He will rest for a little while in England, a country that was always good to him, then to America, and his journey will be ended.

"I've got the unfinished manuscript of his last novel here beside me, a rollicking Irish tale, different from anything he ever wrote before. Stephen thought I was the only person who could finish it, and he was too ill for me to refuse. I don't know what to do about the matter, for I never could work up another man's ideas. Even your vivid imagination could hardly conjecture anything more ghastly than the dying man, lying by an open window overlooking the English channel, relating in a sepulchral whisper the comic situations of his humorous hero so that I might take up the thread of his story.

"From the window beside which I write this I can see down in the valley Ravensbrook House, where Crane used to live and where Harold Frederic, he and I spent many a merry night together. When the Romans occupied Britain, some of their legions, parched with thirst, were wandering about these dry hills with the chance of finding water or perishing. They watched the ravens, and so came to the stream which rises under my place and flows past Stephen's former home; hence the name, Ravensbrook.

"It seems a strange coincidence that the greatest modern writer on war should set himself down where the greatest ancient warrior, Cæsar, probably stopped to quench his thirst.

"Stephen died at three in the morning, the same sinister hour which carried away our friend Frederic nineteen months before. At midnight, in Crane's fourteenth-century house in Sussex, we two tried to lure back the ghost of Frederic into that house of ghosts, and to our company, thinking that if reappearing were ever possible so strenuous a man as Harold would somehow shoulder his way past the guards, but he made no sign. I wonder if the less insistent Stephen will suggest some ingenious method by which the two can pass the barrier. I can imagine Harold cursing on the other side, and welcoming the more subtle assistance of his finely fibred friend.

"I feel like the last of the Three Musketeers, the other two gone down in their duel with Death. I am wondering if, within the next two years, I also shall get the challenge. If so, I shall go to the competing ground the more cheerfully that two such good fellows await the outcome on the other side.

"Ever your friend,

"ROBERT BARR."

The last of the Three Musketeers is gone, now, although he outlived his friends by some years. Robert Barr died in 1912. Perhaps they are still debating a joint return.

There could be, perhaps, no better close for a paper on Stephen Crane than the subjoined paragraph from a letter written by him to a Rochester editor:—

"The one thing that deeply pleases me is the fact that men of sense invariably believe me to be sincere. I know that my work does not amount to a string of dried beans—I always calmly admit it——but I also know that I do the best that is in me without regard to praise or blame. When I was the mark for every humorist in the country, I went ahead; and now when I am the mark for only fifty per cent of the humorists of the country, I go ahead; for I understand that a man is born into the world with his own pair of eyes, and he is not at all responsible for his vision—he is merely responsible for his quality of personal honesty. To keep close to this personal honesty is my supreme ambition."

VINCENT STARRETT.

THE OPEN BOAT

THE OPEN BOAT

A TALE INTENDED TO BE AFTER THE FACT. BEING THE EX-
PERIENCE OF FOUR MEN FROM THE SUNK STEAMER
"COMMODORE."

I

NONE of them knew the color of the sky. Their eyes glanced level, and were fastened upon the waves that swept toward them. These waves were of the hue of slate, save for the tops, which were of foaming white, and all of the men knew the colors of the sea. The horizon narrowed and widened, and dipped and rose, and at all times its edge was jagged with waves that seemed thrust up in points like rocks. Many a man ought to have a bath-tub larger than the boat which here rode upon the sea. These waves were most wrongfully and barbarously abrupt and tall, and each froth-top was a problem in small-boat navigation.

The cook squatted in the bottom and looked with both eyes at the six inches of gunwale which separated him from the ocean. His sleeves were rolled over his fat forearms, and the two flaps of his unbuttoned vest dangled as he bent to bail out the boat. Often he said: "Gawd! That was a narrow clip." As he remarked it he invariably gazed east-ward over the broken sea.

[1] Copyright, 1898, by Doubleday, Page and Company.

The oiler, steering with one of the two oars in the boat, sometimes raised himself suddenly to keep clear of water that swirled in over the stern. It was a thin little oar and it seemed often ready to snap.

The correspondent, pulling at the other oar, watched the waves and wondered why he was there.

The injured captain, lying in the bow, was at this time buried in that profound dejection and indifference which comes, temporarily at least, to even the bravest and most enduring when, willy nilly, the firm fails, the army loses, the ship goes down. The mind of the master of a vessel is rooted deep in the timbers of her, though he commanded for a day or a decade, and this captain had on him the stern impression of a scene in the greys of dawn of seven turned faces, and later a stump of a top-mast with a white ball on it that slashed to and fro at the waves, went low and lower, and down. Thereafter there was something strange in his voice. Although steady, it was deep with mourning, and of a quality beyond oration or tears.

"Keep 'er a little more south, Billie," said he.

" 'A little more south,' sir," said the oiler in the stern.

A seat in this boat was not unlike a seat upon a bucking broncho, and by the same token, a broncho is not much smaller. The craft pranced and reared, and plunged like an animal. As each wave came, and she rose for it, she seemed like a horse making at a fence outrageously high. The manner of her scramble over these walls of water is a mystic thing, and, moreover, at the top of them were ordinarily these problems in white water, the foam racing down from the summit of each wave, requiring a new leap, and a leap from the air. Then, after scornfully bumping a crest, she would slide, and race, and splash down a long incline, and arrive bobbing and nodding in front of the next menace.

A singular disadvantage of the sea lies in the fact that after successfully surmounting one wave you discover that there is another behind it just as important and just as nervously anxious to do something effective in the way of swamping boats. In a ten-foot dingey one can get an idea of the resources of the sea in the line of waves that is not probable to the average experience which is never at sea in a dingey. As each slatey wall of water approached, it shut all else from the view of the men in the boat, and it was not difficult to imagine that this particular wave was the final outburst of the ocean, the last effort of the grim water. There was a terrible grace in the move of the waves, and they came in silence, save for the snarling of the crests.

In the wan light, the faces of the men must have been grey. Their eyes must have glinted in strange ways as they gazed steadily astern. Viewed from a balcony, the whole thing would doubtless have been weirdly picturesque. But the men in the boat had no time to see it, and if they had had leisure there were other things to occupy their minds. The sun swung steadily up the sky, and they knew it was broad day because the color of the sea changed from slate to emerald-green, streaked with amber lights, and the foam was like tumbling snow. The process of the breaking day was unknown to them. They were aware only of this effect upon the color of the waves that rolled toward them.

In disjointed sentences the cook and the correspondent argued as to the difference between a life-saving station and a house of refuge. The cook had said: "There's a house of refuge just north of the Mosquito Inlet Light, and as soon as they see us, they'll come off in their boat and pick us up."

"As soon as who see us?" said the correspondent.

"The crew," said the cook.

"Houses of refuge don't have crews," said the correspondent. "As I understand them, they are only places where clothes and grub are stored for the benefit of shipwrecked people. They don't carry crews."

"Oh, yes, they do," said the cook.

"No, they don't," said the correspondent.

"Well, we're not there yet, anyhow," said the oiler, in the stern.

"Well," said the cook, "perhaps it's not a house of refuge that I'm thinking of as being near Mosquito Inlet Light. Perhaps it's a life-saving station."

"We're not there yet," said the oiler, in the stern.

II

As the boat bounced from the top of each wave, the wind tore through the hair of the hatless men, and as the craft plopped her stern down again the spray splashed past them. The crest of each of these waves was a hill, from the top of which the men surveyed, for a moment, a broad tumultuous expanse, shining and wind-riven. It was probably splendid. It was probably glorious, this play of the free sea, wild with lights of emerald and white and amber.

"Bully good thing it's an on-shore wind," said the cook. "If not, where would we be? Wouldn't have a show."

ed was not apparent to those in her. She seemed just
—ing wallowing, miraculously top-up, at the mercy
—ceans. Occasionally, a great spread of water, like whi
—es, swarmed into her.

—Bail her, cook," said the captain serenely.

—All right, captain," said the cheerful cook.

III

—would be difficult to describe the subtle brotherhood o
—at was here established on the seas. No one said tha
—o. No one mentioned it. But it dwelt in the boat
—h man felt it warm him. They were a captain, a
—cook, and a correspondent, and they were friends
—n a more curiously iron-bound degree than may be

The hurt captain, lying against the water-jar in
—spoke always in a low voice and calmly, but he
—r command a more ready and swiftly obedient crew
—motley three of the dingey. It was more than a
—cognition of what was best for the common safety.
—vas surely in it a quality that was personal and heart-
—And after this devotion to the commander of the boat
—vas this comradeship that the correspondent, for in-
—who had been taught to be cynical of men, knew even
—time was the best experience of his life. But no one
—said that it was so. No one mentioned it.

"I wish we had a sail," remarked the captain. "We might
—y my overcoat on the end of an oar and give you two boys
—chance to rest." So the cook and the correspondent held
—mast and spread wide the overcoat. The oiler steered,
—l the little boat made good way with her new rig. Some-

"That's right," said the correspondent.

The busy oiler nodded his assent.

Then the captain, in the bow, chuckled in a way that expressed humor, contempt, tragedy, all in one. "Do you think we've got much of a show now, boys?" said he.

Whereupon the three were silent, save for a trifle of hemming and hawing. To express any particular optimism at this time they felt to be childish and stupid, but they all doubtless possessed this sense of the situation in their mind. A young man thinks doggedly at such times. On the other hand, the ethics of their condition was decidedly against any open suggestion of hopelessness. So they were silent.

"Oh, well," said the captain, soothing his children, "We'll get ashore all right."

But there was that in his tone which made them think, so the oiler quoth: "Yes! If this wind holds!"

The cook was bailing: "Yes! If we don't catch hell in the surf."

Canton flannel gulls flew near and far. Sometimes they sat down on the sea, near patches of brown seaweed that rolled on the waves with a movement like carpets on a line in a gale. The birds sat comfortably in groups, and they were envied by some in the dingey, for the wrath of the sea was no more to them than it was to a covey of prairie chickens a thousand miles inland. Often they came very close and stared at the men with black bead-like eyes. At these times they were uncanny and sinister in their unblinking scrutiny, and the men hooted angrily at them, telling them to be gone. One came, and evidently decided to alight on the top of the captain's head. The bird flew parallel to the boat and did not circle, but made short sidelong jumps in the air in chicken-fashion. His black eyes were wistfully fixed upon the captain's head. "Ugly brute," said the oiler to the bird. "You look as if you were made with a jack-knife." The cook and the correspondent swore darkly at the creature. The captain naturally wished to knock it away with the end of the heavy painter; but he did not dare do it because anything resembling an emphatic gesture would have capsized this freighted boat, and so with his open hand, the captain gently and carefully waved the gull away. After it had been discouraged from the pursuit the captain breathed easier on account of his hair, and others breathed easier because the bird struck their minds at this time as being somehow grewsome and ominous.

In the meantime the oiler and the correspondent rowed. And also they rowed.

They sat together in the same seat, and each rowed an oar. Then the oiler took both oars; then the correspondent took both oars; then the oiler; then the correspondent. They rowed and they rowed. The very ticklish part of the business was when the time came for the reclining one in the stern to take his turn at the oars. By the very last star of truth, it is easier to steal eggs from under a hen than it was to change seats in the dingey. First the man in the stern slid his hand along the thwart and moved with care, as if he were of Sèvres. Then the man in the rowing seat slid his hand along the other thwart. It was all done with the most extraordinary care. As the two sidled past each other, the whole party kept watchful eyes on the coming wave, and the captain cried: "Look out now! Steady there!"

The brown mats of seaweed that app[...] time were like islands, bits of earth. Th[...] apparently, neither one way nor the other[...] all intents, stationary. They informed the [...] that it was making progress slowly toward the [...]

The captain, rearing cautiously in the bow, a[...] gey soared on a great swell, said that he had see[...] house at Mosquito Inlet. Presently the cook remark[...] had seen it. The correspondent was at the oars [...] for some reason he too wished to look at the lightho[...] his back was toward the far shore and the waves we[...] portant, and for some time he could not seize an oppo[...] to turn his head. But at last there came a wave more [...] than the others, and when at the crest of it he swiftly [...] the western horizon.

"See it?" said the captain.

"No," said the correspondent slowly, "I didn't [...] thing."

"Look again," said the captain. He pointed. "It's [...] in that direction."

At the top of another wave, the correspondent did [...] was bid, and this time his eyes chanced on a small stil[...] on the edge of the swaying horizon. It was precise[...] the point of a pin. It took an anxious eye to find a l[...] house so tiny.

"Think we'll make it, captain?"

"If this wind holds and the boat don't swamp, [...] do much else," said the captain.

The little boat, lifted by each towering sea, an[...] viciously by the crests, made progress that in th[...]

"That's right," said the correspondent.

The busy oiler nodded his assent.

Then the captain, in the bow, chuckled in a way that expressed humor, contempt, tragedy, all in one. "Do you think we've got much of a show now, boys?" said he.

Whereupon the three were silent, save for a trifle of hemming and hawing. To express any particular optimism at this time they felt to be childish and stupid, but they all doubtless possessed this sense of the situation in their mind. A young man thinks doggedly at such times. On the other hand, the ethics of their condition was decidedly against any open suggestion of hopelessness. So they were silent.

"Oh, well," said the captain, soothing his children, "We'll get ashore all right."

But there was that in his tone which made them think, so the oiler quoth: "Yes! If this wind holds!"

The cook was bailing: "Yes! If we don't catch hell in the surf."

Canton flannel gulls flew near and far. Sometimes they sat down on the sea, near patches of brown seaweed that rolled on the waves with a movement like carpets on a line in a gale. The birds sat comfortably in groups, and they were envied by some in the dingey, for the wrath of the sea was no more to them than it was to a covey of prairie chickens a thousand miles inland. Often they came very close and stared at the men with black bead-like eyes. At these times they were uncanny and sinister in their unblinking scrutiny, and the men hooted angrily at them, telling them to be gone. One came, and evidently decided to alight on the top of the captain's head. The bird flew parallel to the boat and did not circle, but made short sidelong jumps in the air in chicken-fashion. His black eyes were wistfully fixed upon the captain's head. "Ugly brute," said the oiler to the bird. "You look as if you were made with a jack-knife." The cook and the correspondent swore darkly at the creature. The captain naturally wished to knock it away with the end of the heavy painter; but he did not dare do it because anything resembling an emphatic gesture would have capsized this freighted boat, and so with his open hand, the captain gently and carefully waved the gull away. After it had been discouraged from the pursuit the captain breathed easier on account of his hair, and others breathed easier because the bird struck their minds at this time as being somehow grewsome and ominous.

In the meantime the oiler and the correspondent rowed. And also they rowed.

They sat together in the same seat, and each rowed an oar. Then the oiler took both oars; then the correspondent took both oars; then the oiler; then the correspondent. They rowed and they rowed. The very ticklish part of the business was when the time came for the reclining one in the stern to take his turn at the oars. By the very last star of truth, it is easier to steal eggs from under a hen than it was to change seats in the dingey. First the man in the stern slid his hand along the thwart and moved with care, as if he were of Sèvres. Then the man in the rowing seat slid his hand along the other thwart. It was all done with the most extraordinary care. As the two sidled past each other, the whole party kept watchful eyes on the coming wave, and the captain cried: "Look out now! Steady there!"

The brown mats of seaweed that appeared from time to time were like islands, bits of earth. They were traveling, apparently, neither one way nor the other. They were, to all intents, stationary. They informed the men in the boat that it was making progress slowly toward the land.

The captain, rearing cautiously in the bow, after the dingey soared on a great swell, said that he had seen the lighthouse at Mosquito Inlet. Presently the cook remarked that he had seen it. The correspondent was at the oars then and for some reason he too wished to look at the lighthouse but his back was toward the far shore and the waves were important, and for some time he could not seize an oppo to turn his head. But at last there came a wave more than the others, and when at the crest of it he swiftly the western horizon.

"See it?" said the captain.

"No," said the correspondent slowly, "I didn't thing."

"Look again," said the captain. He pointed. "It's in that direction."

At the top of another wave, the correspondent did was bid, and this time his eyes chanced on a small stil on the edge of the swaying horizon. It was precise the point of a pin. It took an anxious eye to find a light house so tiny.

"Think we'll make it, captain?"

"If this wind holds and the boat don't swamp, we can't do much else," said the captain.

The little boat, lifted by each towering sea, and splashed viciously by the crests, made progress that in the absence of seaweed was not apparent to those in her. She seemed just a wee thing wallowing, miraculously top-up, at the mercy of five oceans. Occasionally, a great spread of water, like white flames, swarmed into her.

"Bail her, cook," said the captain serenely.

"All right, captain," said the cheerful cook.

III

would be difficult to describe the subtle brotherhood of me   at was here established on the seas. No one said that it   o. No one mentioned it. But it dwelt in the boat,   h man felt it warm him. They were a captain, an   cook, and a correspondent, and they were friends,   n a more curiously iron-bound degree than may be   The hurt captain, lying against the water-jar in   spoke always in a low voice and calmly, but he   r command a more ready and swiftly obedient crew   motley three of the dingey. It was more than a   cognition of what was best for the common safety.   vas surely in it a quality that was personal and heart-   nd after this devotion to the commander of the boat   as this comradeship that the correspondent, for in-   who had been taught to be cynical of men, knew even   time was the best experience of his life. But no one said that it was so. No one mentioned it.

"I wish we had a sail," remarked the captain. "We might try my overcoat on the end of an oar and give you two boys a chance to rest." So the cook and the correspondent held the mast and spread wide the overcoat. The oiler steered, and the little boat made good way with her new rig. Sometimes the oiler had to scull sharply to keep a sea from breaking into the boat, but otherwise sailing was a success.

Meanwhile the lighthouse had been growing slowly larger. It had now almost assumed color, and appeared like a little grey shadow on the sky. The man at the oars could not be prevented from turning his head rather often to try for a glimpse of this little grey shadow.

At last, from the top of each wave the men in the tossing boat could see land. Even as the lighthouse was an upright shadow on the sky, this land seemed but a long black shadow on the sea. It certainly was thinner than paper. "We must be about opposite New Smyrna," said the cook, who had coasted this shore often in schooners. "Captain, by the way, I believe they abandoned that life-saving station there about a year ago."

"Did they?" said the captain.

The wind slowly died away. The cook and the correspondent were not now obliged to slave in order to hold high the oar. But the waves continued their old impetuous swooping at the dingey, and the little craft, no longer under way, struggled woundily over them. The oiler or the correspondent took the oars again.

Shipwrecks are *à propos* of nothing. If men could only train for them and have them occur when the men had reached pink condition, there would be less drowning at sea. Of the four in the dingey none had slept any time worth mentioning for two days and two nights previous to embarking in the dingey, and in the excitement of clambering about the deck of a foundering ship they had also forgotten to eat heartily.

For these reasons, and for others, neither the oiler nor the correspondent was fond of rowing at this time. The correspondent wondered ingenuously how in the name of all that was sane could there be people who thought it amusing to row a boat. It was not an amusement; it was a diabolical punishment, and even a genius of mental aberrations could never conclude that it was anything but a horror to the muscles and a crime against the back. He mentioned to the boat in general how the amusement of rowing struck him, and the weary-faced oiler smiled in full sympathy. Previously to the foundering, by the way, the oiler had worked double-watch in the engine-room of the ship.

"Take her easy, now, boys," said the captain. "Don't spend yourselves. If we have to run a surf you'll need all your strength, because we'll sure have to swim for it. Take your time."

Slowly the land arose from the sea. From a black line it became a line of black and a line of white, trees and sand. Finally, the captain said that he could make out a house on the shore. "That's the house of refuge, sure," said the cook. "They'll see us before long, and come out after us."

The distant lighthouse reared high. "The keeper ought to be able to make us out now, if he's looking through a glass," said the captain. "He'll notify the life-saving people."

"None of those other boats could have got ashore to give word of the wreck," said the oiler, in a low voice. "Else the lifeboat would be out hunting us."

Slowly and beautifully the land loomed out of the sea. The wind came again. It had veered from the north-east to the south-east. Finally, a new sound struck the ears of the men in the boat. It was the low thunder of the surf on the shore. "We'll never be able to make the lighthouse now," said the captain. "Swing her head a little more north, Billie," said he.

" 'A little more north,' sir," said the oiler.

Whereupon the little boat turned her nose once more down the wind, and all but the oarsman watched the shore grow. Under the influence of this expansion doubt and direful apprehension was leaving the minds of the men. The management of the boat was still most absorbing, but it could not prevent a quiet cheerfulness. In an hour, perhaps, they would be ashore.

Their backbones had become thoroughly used to balancing in the boat, and they now rode this wild colt of a dingey like circus men. The correspondent thought that he had been drenched to the skin, but happening to feel in the top pocket of his coat, he found therein eight cigars. Four of them were soaked with sea-water; four were perfectly scathless. After a search, somebody produced three dry matches, and thereupon the four waifs rode impudently in their little boat, and with an assurance of an impending rescue shining in their eyes, puffed at the big cigars and judged well and ill of all men. Everybody took a drink of water.

IV

"Cook," remarked the captain, "there don't seem to be any signs of life about your house of refuge."

"No," replied the cook. "Funny they don't see us!"

A broad stretch of lowly coast lay before the eyes of the men. It was of dunes topped with dark vegetation. The roar of the surf was plain, and sometimes they could see the white lip of a wave as it spun up the beach. A tiny house was blocked out black upon the sky. Southward, the slim lighthouse lifted its little grey length.

Tide, wind, and waves were swinging the dingey northward. "Funny they don't see us," said the men.

The surf's roar was here dulled, but its tone was, nevertheless, thunderous and mighty. As the boat swam over the great rollers, the men sat listening to this roar. "We'll swamp sure," said everybody.

It is fair to say here that there was not a life-saving station within twenty miles in either direction, but the men did not know this fact, and in consequence they made dark and opprobrious remarks concerning the eyesight of the nation's life-savers. Four scowling men sat in the dingey and surpassed records in the invention of epithets.

"Funny they don't see us."

The lightheartedness of a former time had completely faded. To their sharpened minds it was easy to conjure pictures of all kinds of incompetency and blindness and, indeed, cowardice. There was the shore of the populous land, and it was bitter and bitter to them that from it came no sign.

"Well," said the captain, ultimately, "I suppose we'll have to make a try for ourselves. If we stay out here too long, we'll none of us have strength left to swim after the boat swamps."

And so the oiler, who was at the oars, turned the boat straight for the shore. There was a sudden tightening of muscle. There was some thinking.

"If we don't all get ashore——" said the captain. "If we

don't all get ashore, I suppose you fellows know where to send news of my finish?"

They then briefly exchanged some addresses and admonitions. As for the reflections of the men, there was a great deal of rage in them. Perchance they might be formulated thus: "If I am going to be drowned—if I am going to be drowned—if I am going to be drowned, why, in the name of the seven mad gods who rule the sea, was I allowed to come thus far and contemplate sand and trees? Was I brought here merely to have my nose dragged away as I was about to nibble the sacred cheese of life? It is preposterous. If this old ninny-woman, Fate, cannot do better than this, she should be deprived of the management of men's fortunes. She is an old hen who knows not her intention. If she has decided to drown me, why did she not do it in the beginning and save me all this trouble? The whole affair is absurd. . . But no, she cannot mean to drown me. She dare not drown me. She cannot drown me. Not after all this work." Afterward the man might have had an impulse to shake his fist at the clouds: "Just you drown me, now, and then hear what I call you!"

The billows that came at this time were more formidable. They seemed always just about to break and roll over the little boat in a turmoil of foam. There was a preparatory and long growl in the speech of them. No mind unused to the sea would have concluded that the dingey could ascend these sheer heights in time. The shore was still afar. The oiler was a wily surfman. "Boys," he said swiftly, "she won't live three minutes more, and we're too far out to swim. Shall I take her to sea again, captain?"

"Yes! Go ahead!" said the captain.

This oiler, by a series of quick miracles, and fast and steady oarsmanship, turned the boat in the middle of the surf and took her safely to sea again.

There was a considerable silence as the boat bumped over the furrowed sea to deeper water. Then somebody in gloom spoke. "Well, anyhow, they must have seen us from the shore by now."

The gulls went in slanting flight up the wind toward the grey desolate east. A squall, marked by dingy clouds, and clouds brick-red, like smoke from a burning building, appeared from the south-east.

"What do you think of those life-saving people? Ain't they peaches?'

"Funny they haven't seen us."

"Maybe they think we're out here for sport! Maybe they think we're fishin'. Maybe they think we're damned fools."

It was a long afternoon. A changed tide tried to force them southward, but the wind and wave said northward. Far ahead, where coast-line, sea, and sky formed their mighty angle, there were little dots which seemed to indicate a city on the shore.

"St. Augustine?"

The captain shook his head. "Too near Mosquito Inlet."

And the oiler rowed, and then the correspondent rowed. Then the oiler rowed. It was a weary business. The human back can become the seat of more aches and pains than are registered in books for the composite anatomy of a regiment. It is a limited area, but it can become the theatre of innumerable muscular conflicts, tangles, wrenches, knots, and other comforts.

"Did you ever like to row, Billie?" asked the correspondent.

"No," said the oiler. "Hang it!"

When one exchanged the rowing-seat for a place in the bottom of the boat, he suffered a bodily depression that caused him to be careless of everything save an obligation to wiggle one finger. There was cold sea-water swashing to and fro in the boat, and he lay in it. His head, pillowed on a thwart, was within an inch of the swirl of a wave crest, and sometimes a particularly obstreperous sea came in-board and drenched him once more. But these matters did not annoy him. It is almost certain that if the boat had capsized he would have tumbled comfortably out upon the ocean as if he felt sure that it was a great soft mattress.

"Look! There's a man on the shore!"

"Where?"

"There! See 'im? See 'im?"

"Yes, sure! He's walking along."

"Now he's stopped. Look! He's facing us!"

"He's waving at us!"

"So he is! By thunder!"

"Ah, now we're all right! Now we're all right! There'll be a boat out here for us in half-an-hour."

"He's going on. He's running. He's going up to that house there."

The remote beach seemed lower than the sea, and it required a searching glance to discern the little black figure. The captain saw a floating stick and they rowed to it. A bath-towel was by some weird chance in the boat, and, tying this on the stick, the captain waved it. The oarsman did not dare turn his head, so he was obliged to ask questions.

"What's he doing now?"

"He's standing still again. He's looking, I think. . . . . There he goes again. Toward the house. . . . Now he's stopped again."

"Is he waving at us?"

"No, not now! he was, though."

"Look! There comes another man!"

"He's running."

"Look at him go, would you."

"Why, he's on a bicycle. Now he's met the other man. They're both waving at us. Look!"

"There comes something up the beach."

"What the devil is that thing?"

"Why it looks like a boat."

"Why, certainly it's a boat."

"No, it's on wheels."

"Yes, so it is. Well, that must be the life-boat. They drag them along shore on a wagon."

"That's the life-boat, sure."

"No, by ———, it's—it's an omnibus."

"I tell you it's a life-boat."

"It is not! It's an omnibus. I can see it plain. See? One of these big hotel omnibuses."

"By thunder, you're right. It's an omnibus, sure as fate. What do you suppose they are doing with an omnibus? Maybe they are going around collecting the life-crew, hey?"

"That's it, likely. Look! There's a fellow waving a

little black flag. He's standing on the steps of the omnibus. There come those other two fellows. Now they're all talking together. Look at the fellow with the flag. Maybe he ain't waving it."

"That ain't a flag, is it? That's his coat. Why, certainly, that's his coat."

"So it is. It's his coat. He's taken it off and is waving it around his head. But would you look at him swing it."

"Oh, say, there isn't any life-saving station there. That's just a winter resort hotel omnibus that has brought over some of the boarders to see us drown."

"What's that idiot with the coat mean? What's he signaling, anyhow?"

"It looks as if he were trying to tell us to go north. There must be a life-saving station up there."

"No! He thinks we're fishing. Just giving us a merry hand. See? Ah, there, Willie!"

"Well, I wish I could make something out of those signals. What do you suppose he means?"

"He don't mean anything. He's just playing."

"Well, if he'd just signal us to try the surf again, or to go to sea and wait, or go north, or go south, or go to hell— there would be some reason in it. But look at him. He just stands there and keeps his coat revolving like a wheel. The ass!"

"There come more people."

"Now there's quite a mob. Look! Isn't that a boat?"

"Where? Oh, I see where you mean. No, that's no boat."

"That fellow is still waving his coat."

"He must think we like to see him do that. Why don't he quit it? It don't mean anything."

"I don't know. I think he is trying to make us go north. It must be that there's a life-saving station there somewhere."

"Say, he ain't tired yet. Look at 'im wave."

"Wonder how long he can keep that up. He's been revolving his coat ever since he caught sight of us. He's an idiot. Why aren't they getting men to bring a boat out? A fishing boat—one of those big yawls—could come out here all right. Why don't he do something?"

"Oh, it's all right, now."

"They'll have a boat out here for us in less than no time, now that they've seen us."

A faint yellow tone came into the sky over the low land. The shadows on the sea slowly deepened. The wind bore coldness with it, and the men began to shiver.

"Holy smoke!" said one, allowing his voice to express his impious mood, "if we keep on monkeying out here! If we've got to flounder out here all night!"

"Oh, we'll never have to stay here all night! Don't you worry. They've seen us now, and it won't be long before they'll come chasing out after us."

The shore grew dusky. The man waving a coat blended gradually into this gloom, and it swallowed in the same manner the omnibus and the group of people. The spray, when it dashed uproariously over the side, made the voyagers shrink and swear like men who were being branded.

"I'd like to catch the chump who waved the coat. I feel like soaking him one, just for luck."

"Why? What did he do?"

"Oh, nothing, but then he seemed so damned cheerful."

In the meantime the oiler rowed, and then the correspondent rowed, and then the oiler rowed. Grey-faced and bowed forward, they mechanically, turn by turn, plied the leaden oars. The form of the lighthouse had vanished from the southern horizon, but finally a pale star appeared, just lifting from the sea. The streaked saffron in the west passed before the all-merging darkness, and the sea to the east was black. The land had vanished, and was expressed only by the low and drear thunder of the surf.

"If I am going to be drowned—if I am going to be drowned—if I am going to be drowned, why, in the name of the seven mad gods who rule the sea, was I allowed to come thus far and contemplate sand and trees? Was I brought here merely to have my nose dragged away as I was about to nibble the sacred cheese of life?"

The patient captain, drooped over the water-jar, was sometimes obliged to speak to the oarsman.

"Keep her head up! Keep her head up!"

" 'Keep her head up,' sir." The voices were weary and low.

This was surely a quiet evening. All save the oarsman lay heavily and listlessly in the boat's bottom. As for him, his eyes were just capable of noting the tall black waves that swept forward in a most sinister silence, save for an occasional subdued growl of a crest.

The cook's head was on a thwart, and he looked without interest at the water under his nose. He was deep in other scenes. Finally he spoke. "Billie," he murmured, dreamfully, "what kind of pie do you like best?"

V

"PIE," said the oiler and the correspondent, agitatedly.
"Don't talk about those things, blast you!"

"Well," said the cook, "I was just thinking about ham
sandwiches, and——"

A night on the sea in an open boat is a long night. As
darkness settled finally, the shine of the light, lifting from
the sea in the south, changed to full gold. On the northern
horizon a new light appeared, a small bluish gleam on the
edge of the waters. These two lights were the furniture of
the world. Otherwise there was nothing but waves.

Two men huddled in the stern, and distances were so magnificent in the dingey that the rower was enabled to keep
his feet partly warmed by thrusting them under his companions. Their legs indeed extended far under the rowing-
seat until they touched the feet of the captain forward.
Sometimes, despite the efforts of the tired oarsman, a wave
came piling into the boat, an icy wave of the night, and the
chilling water soaked them anew. They would twist their
bodies for a moment and groan, and sleep the dead sleep
once more, while the water in the boat gurgled about them
as the craft rocked.

The plan of the oiler and the correspondent was for one
to row until he lost the ability, and then arouse
the other from his sea-water couch in the bottom of
the boat.

The oiler plied the oars until his head drooped forward,
and the overpowering sleep blinded him. And he rowed yet
afterward. Then he touched a man in the bottom of the

boat, and called his name. "Will you spell me for a little while?" he said, meekly.

"Sure, Billie," said the correspondent, awakening and dragging himself to a sitting position. They exchanged places carefully, and the oiler, cuddling down in the sea-water at the cook's side, seemed to go to sleep instantly.

The particular violence of the sea had ceased. The waves came without snarling. The obligation of the man at the oars was to keep the boat headed so that the tilt of the rollers would not capsize her, and to preserve her from filling when the crests rushed past. The black waves were silent and hard to be seen in the darkness. Often one was almost upon the boat before the oarsman was aware.

In a low voice the correspondent addressed the captain. He was not sure that the captain was awake, although this iron man seemed to be always awake. "Captain, shall I keep her making for that light north, sir?"

The same steady voice answered him. "Yes. Keep it about two points off the port bow."

The cook had tied a life-belt around himself in order to get even the warmth which this clumsy cork contrivance could donate, and he seemed almost stove-like when a rower, whose teeth invariably chattered wildly as soon as he ceased his labor, dropped down to sleep.

The correspondent, as he rowed, looked down at the two men sleeping under-foot. The cook's arm was around the oiler's shoulders, and, with their fragmentary clothing and haggard faces, they were the babes of the sea, a grotesque rendering of the old babes in the wood.

Later he must have grown stupid at his work, for suddenly there was a growling of water, and a crest came with a roar and a swash into the boat, and it was a wonder that it did not set the cook afloat in his life-belt. The cook continued to sleep, but the oiler sat up, blinking his eyes and shaking with the new cold.

"Oh, I'm awful sorry, Billie," said the correspondent contritely.

"That's all right, old boy," said the oiler, and lay down again and was asleep.

Presently it seemed that even the captain dozed, and the correspondent thought that he was the one man afloat on all the oceans. The wind had a voice as it came over the waves, and it was sadder than the end.

There was a long, loud swishing astern of the boat, and a gleaming trail of phosphorescence, like blue flame, was furrowed on the black waters. It might have been made by a monstrous knife.

Then there came a stillness, while the correspondent breathed with the open mouth and looked at the sea.

Suddenly there was another swish and another long flash of bluish light, and this time it was alongside the boat, and might almost have been reached with an oar. The correspondent saw an enormous fin speed like a shadow through the water, hurling the crystalline spray and leaving the long glowing trail.

The correspondent looked over his shoulder at the captain. His face was hidden, and he seemed to be asleep. He looked at the babes of the sea. They certainly were asleep. So, being bereft of sympathy, he leaned a little way to one side and swore softly into the sea.

But the thing did not then leave the vicinity of the boat. Ahead or astern, on one side or the other, at intervals long or short, fled the long sparkling streak, and there was to be heard the whirroo of the dark fin. The speed and power of the thing was greatly to be admired. It cut the water like a gigantic and keen projectile.

The presence of this biding thing did not affect the man with the same horror that it would if he had been a picnicker. He simply looked at the sea dully and swore in an undertone.

Nevertheless, it is true that he did not wish to be alone. He wished one of his companions to awaken by chance and keep him company with it. But the captain hung motionless over the water-jar, and the oiler and the cook in the bottom of the boat were plunged in slumber.

VI

"If I am going to be drowned—if I am going to be drowned—if I am going to be drowned, why, in the name of the seven mad gods who rule the sea, was I allowed to come thus far and contemplate sand and trees?"

During this dismal night, it may be remarked that a man would conclude that it was really the intention of the seven mad gods to drown him, despite the abominable injustice of it. For it was certainly an abominable injustice to drown a man who had worked so hard, so hard. The man felt it would be a crime most unnatural. Other people had drowned at sea since galleys swarmed with painted sails, but still——

When it occurs to a man that nature does not regard him

as important, and that she feels she would not maim the
universe by disposing of him, he at first wishes to throw
bricks at the temple, and he hates deeply the fact that there
are no brick and no temples. Any visible expression of
nature would surely be pelleted with his jeers.

Then, if there be no tangible thing to hoot he feels, perhaps, the desire to confront a personification and indulge in
pleas, bowed to one knee, and with hands supplicant, saying: "Yes, but I love myself."

A high cold star on a winter's night is the word he feels
that she says to him. Thereafter he knows the pathos of
his situation.

The men in the dingey had not discussed these matters,
but each had, no doubt, reflected upon them in silence and
according to his mind. There was seldom any expression
upon their faces save the general one of complete weariness.
Speech was devoted to the business of the boat.

To chime the notes of his emotion, a verse mysteriously
entered the correspondent's head. He had even forgotten
that he had forgotten this verse, but it suddenly was in his
mind.

"A soldier of the Legion lay dying in Algiers,
  There was a lack of woman's nursing, there was dearth of
    woman's tears;
  But a comrade stood beside him, and he took that comrade's
    hand,
  And he said: 'I shall never see my own, my native land.'"

In his childhood, the correspondent had been made ac-
quainted with the fact that a soldier of the Legion lay dying
in Algiers, but he had never regarded the fact as important.

Myriads of his school-fellows had informed him of the soldier's plight, but the dinning had naturally ended by making him perfectly indifferent. He had never considered it his affair that a soldier of the Legion lay dying in Algiers, nor had it appeared to him as a matter for sorrow. It was less to him than the breaking of a pencil's point.

Now, however, it quaintly came to him as a human, living thing. It was no longer merely a picture of a few throes in the breast of a poet, meanwhile drinking tea and warming his feet at the grate; it was an actuality—stern, mournful, and fine.

The correspondent plainly saw the soldier. He lay on the sand with his feet out straight and still. While his pale left hand was upon his chest in an attempt to thwart the going of his life, the blood came between his fingers. In the far Algerian distance, a city of low square forms was set against a sky that was faint with the last sunset hues. The correspondent, plying the oars and dreaming of the slow and slower movements of the lips of the soldier, was moved by a profound and perfectly impersonal comprehension. He was sorry for the soldier of the Legion who lay dying in Algiers.

The thing which had followed the boat and waited, had evidently grown bored at the delay. There was no longer to be heard the slash of the cut-water, and there was no longer the flame of the long trail. The light in the north still glimmered, but it was apparently no nearer to the boat. Sometimes the boom of the surf rang in the correspondent's ears, and he turned the craft seaward then and rowed harder. Southward, some one had evidently built a watch-fire on the beach. It was too low and too far to be seen, but it made a shimmering, roseate reflection upon the bluff back of it, and this could be discerned from the boat. The wind came stronger, and sometimes a wave suddenly raged out like a mountain-cat, and there was to be seen the sheen and sparkle of a broken crest.

The captain, in the bow, moved on his water-jar and sat erect. "Pretty long night," he observed to the correspondent. He looked at the shore. "Those life-saving people take their time."

"Did you see that shark playing around?"

"Yes, I saw him. He was a big fellow, all right."

"Wish I had known you were awake."

Later the correspondent spoke into the bottom of the boat. "Billie!" There was a slow and gradual disentanglement. "Billie, will you spell me?"

"Sure," said the oiler.

As soon as the correspondent touched the cold comfortable sea-water in the bottom of the boat, and had huddled close to the cook's life-belt he was deep in sleep, despite the fact that his teeth played all the popular airs. This sleep was so good to him that it was but a moment before he heard a voice call his name in a tone that demonstrated the last stages of exhaustion. "Will you spell me?"

"Sure, Billie."

The light in the north had mysteriously vanished, but the correspondent took his course from the wide-awake captain.

Later in the night they took the boat farther out to sea, and the captain directed the cook to take one oar at the stern and keep the boat facing the seas. He was to call

out if he should hear the thunder of the surf. This plan
enabled the oiler and the correspondent to get respite together. "We'll give those boys a chance to get into shape
again," said the captain. They curled down and, after a
few preliminary chatterings and trembles, slept once more
the dead sleep. Neither knew they had bequeathed to the
cook the company of another shark, or perhaps the same
shark.

As the boat caroused on the waves, spray occasionally
bumped over the side and gave them a fresh soaking, but
this had no power to break their repose. The ominous slash
of the wind and the water affected them as it would have
affected mummies.

"Boys," said the cook, with the notes of every reluctance
in his voice, "she's drifted in pretty close. I guess one of
you had better take her to sea again." The correspondent,
aroused, heard the crash of the toppled crests.

As he was rowing, the captain gave him some whisky-and-
water, and this steadied the chills out of him. "If I ever get
ashore and anybody shows me even a photograph of an
oar——"

At last there was a short conversation.

"Billie. . . . Billie, will you spell me?"

"Sure," said the oiler.

VII

WHEN the correspondent again opened his eyes, the sea
and the sky were each of the grey hue of the dawning.
Later, carmine and gold was painted upon the waters. The

morning appeared finally, in its splendor, with a sky of
pure blue, and the sunlight flamed on the tips of the waves.

On the distant dunes were set many little black cottages,
and a tall white windmill reared above them.   No man, nor
dog, nor bicycle appeared on the beach.   The cottages might
have formed a deserted village.

The voyagers scanned the shore.   A conference was held
in the boat.   "Well," said the captain, "if no help is coming
we might better try a run through the surf right away.   If
we stay out here much longer we will be too weak to do anything for ourselves at all."   The others silently acquiesced in
this reasoning.   The boat was headed for the beach.   The
correspondent wondered if none ever ascended the tall wind-
tower, and if then they never looked seaward.   This tower
was a giant, standing with its back to the plight of the ants.
It represented in a degree, to the correspondent, the serenity
of nature amid the struggles of the individual—nature in the
wind, and nature in the vision of men.   She did not seem
cruel to him then, nor beneficent, nor treacherous, nor wise.
But she was indifferent, flatly indifferent.   It is, perhaps,
plausible that a man in this situation, impressed with the
unconcern of the universe, should see the innumerable flaws
of his life, and have them taste wickedly in his mind and
wish for another chance.   A distinction between right and
wrong seems absurdly clear to him, then, in this new ignorance of the grave-edge, and he understands that if he were
given another opportunity he would mend his conduct and
his words, and be better and brighter during an introduction
or at a tea.

"Now, boys," said the captain, "she is going to swamp,

sure. All we can do is to work her in as far as possible, and then when she swamps, pile out and scramble for the beach. Keep cool now, and don't jump until she swamps sure."

The oiler took the oars. Over his shoulders he scanned the surf. "Captain," he said, "I think I'd better bring her about, and keep her head-on to the seas and back her in."

"All right, Billie," said the captain. "Back her in." The oiler swung the boat then and, seated in the stern, the cook and the correspondent were obliged to look over their shoulders to contemplate the lonely and indifferent shore.

The monstrous in-shore rollers heaved the boat high until the men were again enabled to see the white sheets of water scudding up the slanted beach. "We won't get in very close," said the captain. Each time a man could wrest his attention from the rollers, he turned his glance toward the shore, and in the expression of the eyes during this contemplation there was a singular quality. The correspondent, observing the others, knew that they were not afraid, but the full meaning of their glances was shrouded.

As for himself, he was too tired to grapple fundamentally with the fact. He tried to coerce his mind into thinking of it, but the mind was dominated at this time by the muscles, and the muscles said they did not care. It merely occurred to him that if he should drown it would be a shame.

There were no hurried words, no pallor, no plain agitation. The men simply looked at the shore. "Now, remember to get well clear of the boat when you jump," said the captain.

Seaward the crest of a roller suddenly fell with a thunderous crash, and the long white comber came roaring down upon the boat.

"Steady now," said the captain. The men were silent. They turned their eyes from the shore to the comber and waited. The boat slid up the incline, leaped at the furious top, bounced over it, and swung down the long back of the wave. Some water had been shipped and the cook bailed it out.

But the next crest crashed also. The tumbling, boiling flood of white water caught the boat and whirled it almost perpendicular. Water swarmed in from all sides. The correspondent had his hands on the gunwale at this time, and when the water entered at that place he swiftly withdrew his fingers, as if he objected to wetting them.

The little boat, drunken with this weight of water, reeled and snuggled deeper into the sea.

"Bail her out, cook! Bail her out," said the captain.

"All right, captain," said the cook.

"Now, boys, the next one will do for us, sure," said the oiler. "Mind to jump clear of the boat."

The third wave moved forward, huge, furious, implacable. It fairly swallowed the dingey, and almost simultaneously the men tumbled into the sea. A piece of lifebelt had lain in the bottom of the boat, and as the correspondent went overboard he held this to his chest with his left hand.

The January water was icy, and he reflected immediately that it was colder than he had expected to find it on the coast of Florida. This appeared to his dazed mind as a fact important enough to be noted at the time. The coldness of the water was sad; it was tragic. This fact was somehow so mixed and confused with his opinion of his own situation that it seemed almost a proper reason for tears. The water was cold.

When he came to the surface he was conscious of little but the noisy water. Afterward he saw his companions in the sea. The oiler was ahead in the race. He was swimming strongly and rapidly. Off to the correspondent's left, the cook's great white and corked back bulged out of the water, and in the rear the captain was hanging with his one good hand to the keel of the overturned dingey.

There is a certain immovable quality to a shore, and the correspondent wondered at it amid the confusion of the sea.

It seemed also very attractive, but the correspondent knew that it was a long journey, and he paddled leisurely. The piece of life-preserver lay under him, and sometimes he whirled down the incline of a wave as if he were on a hand-sled.

But finally he arrived at a place in the sea where travel was beset with difficulty. He did not pause swimming to inquire what manner of current had caught him, but there his progress ceased. The shore was set before him like a bit of scenery on a stage, and he looked at it and understood with his eyes each detail of it.

As the cook passed, much farther to the left, the captain was calling to him, "Turn over on your back, cook! Turn over on your back and use the oar."

"All right, sir." The cook turned on his back, and, paddling with an oar, went ahead as if he were a canoe.

Presently the boat also passed to the left of the correspondent with the captain clinging with one hand to the keel. He would have appeared like a man raising himself to look over a board fence, if it were not for the extraordinary gymnastics of the boat. The correspondent marvelled that the captain could still hold to it.

They passed on, nearer to shore—the oiler, the cook, the captain—and following them went the water-jar, bouncing gaily over the seas.

The correspondent remained in the grip of this strange new enemy—a current. The shore, with its white slope of sand and its green bluff, topped with little silent cottages, was spread like a picture before him. It was very near to him then, but he was impressed as one who in a gallery looks at a scene from Brittany or Holland.

He thought: "I am going to drown? Can it be possible? Can it be possible? Can it be possible?" Perhaps an individual must consider his own death to be the final phenomenon of nature.

But later a wave perhaps whirled him out of this small, deadly current, for he found suddenly that he could again make progress toward the shore. Later still, he was aware that the captain, clinging with one hand to the keel of the dingey, had his face turned away from the shore and toward him, and was calling his name. "Come to the boat! Come to the boat!"

In his struggle to reach the captain and the boat, he reflected that when one gets properly wearied, drowning must really be a comfortable arrangement, a cessation of hostilities accompanied by a large degree of relief, and he was glad of it, for the main thing in his mind for some months had been horror of the temporary agony. He did not wish to be hurt.

Presently he saw a man running along the shore. He was undressing with most remarkable speed. Coat, trousers, shirt, everything flew magically off him.

"Come to the boat," called the captain.

"All right, captain." As the correspondent paddled, he saw the captain let himself down to bottom and leave the boat. Then the correspondent performed his one little marvel of the voyage. A large wave caught him and flung him with ease and supreme speed completely over the boat and far beyond it. It struck him even then as an event in gymnastics, and a true miracle of the sea. An over-turned boat in the surf is not a plaything to a swimming man.

The correspondent arrived in water that reached only to his waist, but his condition did not enable him to stand for more than a moment. Each wave knocked him into a heap, and the under-tow pulled at him.

Then he saw the man who had been running and undressing, and undressing and running, come bounding into the water. He dragged ashore the cook, and then waded towards the captain, but the captain waved him away, and sent him to the correspondent. He was naked, naked as a tree in winter, but a halo was about his head, and he shone like a saint. He gave a strong pull, and a long drag, and a bully heave at the correspondent's hand. The correspondent, schooled in the minor formulæ, said: "Thanks, old man." But suddenly the man cried: "What's that?" He pointed a swift finger. The correspondent said: "Go."

In the shallows, face downward, lay the oiler. His forehead touched sand that was periodically, between each wave, clear of the sea.

The correspondent did not know all that transpired afterward. When he achieved safe ground he fell, striking the sand with each particular part of his body. It was as if he had dropped from a roof, but the thud was grateful to him.

It seems that instantly the beach was populated with men with blankets, clothes, and flasks, and women with coffeepots and all the remedies sacred to their minds. The welcome of the land to the men from the sea was warm and generous, but a still and dripping shape was carried slowly up the beach, and the land's welcome for it could only be the different and sinister hospitality of the grave.

When it came night, the white waves paced to and fro in the moonlight, and the wind brought the sound of the great sea's voice to the men on shore, and they felt that they could then be interpreters.

THE RELUCTANT VOYAGERS

THE RELUCTANT VOYAGERS

THE RELUCTANT VOYAGERS

CHAPTER I

Two men sat by the sea waves.

"Well, I know I'm not handsome," said one gloomily. He was poking holes in the sand with a discontented cane.

The companion was watching the waves play. He seemed overcome with perspiring discomfort as a man who is resolved to set another man right.

Suddenly his mouth turned into a straight line.

"To be sure you are not," he cried vehemently.

"You look like thunder. I do not desire to be unpleasant, but I must assure you that your freckled skin continually reminds spectators of white wall paper with gilt roses on it. The top of your head looks like a little wooden plate. And your figure—heavens!"

For a time they were silent. They stared at the waves that purred near their feet like sleepy sea-kittens.

Finally the first man spoke.

"Well," said he, defiantly, "what of it?"

"What of it?" exploded the other. "Why, it means that you'd look like blazes in a bathing-suit."

They were again silent. The freckled man seemed ashamed. His tall companion glowered at the scenery.

59

"I am decided," said the freckled man suddenly. He got boldly up from the sand and strode away. The tall man followed, walking sarcastically and glaring down at the round, resolute figure before him.

A bath-clerk was looking at the world with superior eyes through a hole in a board. To him the freckled man made application, waving his hands over his person in illustration of a snug fit. The bath-clerk thought profoundly. Eventually, he handed out a blue bundle with an air of having phenomenally solved the freckled man's dimensions.

The latter resumed his resolute stride.

"See here," said the tall man, following him, "I bet you've got a regular toga, you know. That fellow couldn't tell——"

"Yes, he could," interrupted the freckled man, "I saw correct mathematics in his eyes."

"Well, supposin' he has missed your size. Supposin'——"

"Tom," again interrupted the other, "produce your proud clothes and we'll go in."

The tall man swore bitterly. He went to one of a row of little wooden boxes and shut himself in it. His companion repaired to a similar box.

At first he felt like an opulent monk in a too-small cell, and he turned round two or three times to see if he could. He arrived finally into his bathing-dress. Immediately he dropped gasping upon a three-cornered bench. The suit fell in folds about his reclining form. There was silence, save for the caressing calls of the waves without.

Then he heard two shoes drop on the floor in one of the little coops. He began to clamor at the boards like a penitent at an unforgiving door.

"Tom," called he, "Tom——"

A voice of wrath, muffled by cloth, came through the walls. "You go t' blazes!"

The freckled man began to groan, taking the occupants of the entire row of coops into his confidence.

"Stop your noise," angrily cried the tall man from his hidden den. "You rented the bathing-suit, didn't you? Then——"

"It ain't a bathing-suit," shouted the freckled man at the boards. "It's an auditorium, a ballroom, or something. It ain't a bathing-suit."

The tall man came out of his box. His suit looked like blue skin. He walked with grandeur down the alley between the rows of coops. Stopping in front of his friend's door, he rapped on it with passionate knuckles.

"Come out of there, y' ol' fool," said he, in an enraged whisper. "It's only your accursed vanity. Wear it anyhow. What difference does it make? I never saw such a vain ol' idiot!"

As he was storming the door opened, and his friend confronted him. The tall man's legs gave way, and he fell against the opposite door.

The freckled man regarded him sternly.

"You're an ass," he said.

His back curved in scorn. He walked majestically down the alley. There was pride in the way his chubby feet patted the boards. The tall man followed, weakly, his eyes riveted upon the figure ahead.

As a disguise the freckled man had adopted the stomach of importance. He moved with an air of some sort of procession, across a board walk, down some steps, and out upon the sand.

There was a pug dog and three old women on a bench, a man and a maid with a book and a parasol, a seagull drifting high in the wind, and a distant, tremendous meeting of sea and sky. Down on the wet sand stood a girl being wooed by the breakers.

The freckled man moved with stately tread along the beach. The tall man, numb with amazement, came in the rear. They neared the girl.

Suddenly the tall man was seized with convulsions. He laughed, and the girl turned her head.

She perceived the freckled man in the bathing-suit. An expression of wonderment overspread her charming face. It changed in a moment to a pearly smile.

This smile seemed to smite the freckled man. He obviously tried to swell and fit his suit. Then he turned a shrivelling glance upon his companion, and fled up the beach. The tall man ran after him, pursuing with mocking cries that tingled his flesh like stings of insects. He seemed to be trying to lead the way out of the world. But at last he stopped and faced about.

"Tom Sharp," said he, between his clenched teeth, "you are an unutterable wretch! I could grind your bones under my heel."

The tall man was in a trance, with glazed eyes fixed on the bathing-dress. He seemed to be murmuring: "Oh, good Lord! Oh, good Lord! I never saw such a suit!"

The freckled man made the gesture of an assassin.

"Tom Sharp, you——"

The other was still murmuring: "Oh, good Lord! I never saw such a suit! I never——"

The freckled man ran down into the sea.

CHAPTER II

THE cool, swirling waters took his temper from him, and it became a thing that is lost in the ocean. The tall man floundered in, and the two forgot and rollicked in the waves.

The freckled man, in endeavoring to escape from mankind, had left all save a solitary fisherman under a large hat, and three boys in bathing-dress, laughing and splashing upon a raft made of old spars.

The two men swam softly over the ground swells.

The three boys dived from their raft, and turned their jolly faces shorewards. It twisted slowly around and around, and began to move seaward on some unknown voyage. The freckled man laid his face to the water and swam toward the raft with a practised stroke. The tall man followed, his bended arm appearing and disappearing with the precision of machinery.

The craft crept away, slowly and wearily, as if luring. The little wooden plate on the freckled man's head looked at the shore like a round, brown eye, but his gaze was fixed on the raft that slyly appeared to be waiting. The tall man used the little wooden plate as a beacon.

At length the freckled man reached the raft and climbed aboard. He lay down on his back and puffed. His bathing-dress spread about him like a dead balloon. The tall man came, snorted, shook his tangled locks and lay down by the side of his companion.

They were overcome with a delicious drowsiness. The planks of the raft seemed to fit their tired limbs. They gazed dreamily up into the vast sky of summer.

"This is great," said the tall man. His companion grunted blissfully.

Gentle hands from the sea rocked their craft and lulled them to peace. Lapping waves sang little rippling sea-songs about them. The two men issued contented groans.

"Tom," said the freckled man.

"What?" said the other.

"This is great."

They lay and thought.

A fish-hawk, soaring, suddenly, turned and darted at the waves. The tall man indolently twisted his head and watched the bird plunge its claws into the water. It heavily arose with a silver gleaming fish.

"That bird has got his feet wet again. It's a shame," murmured the tall man sleepily. "He must suffer from an endless cold in the head. He should wear rubber boots. They'd look great, too. If I was him, I'd—Great Scott!"

He had partly arisen, and was looking at the shore.

He began to scream. "Ted! Ted! Ted! Look!"

"What's matter?" dreamily spoke the freckled man. "You remind me of when I put the bird-shot in your leg." He giggled softly.

The agitated tall man made a gesture of supreme eloquence. His companion up-reared and turned a startled gaze shoreward.

"Lord!" he roared, as if stabbed.

The land was a long, brown streak with a rim of green, in which sparkled the tin roofs of huge hotels. The hands from the sea had pushed them away. The two men sprang erect, and did a little dance of perturbation.

"What shall we do? What shall we do?" moaned the freckled man, wriggling fantastically in his dead balloon.

The changing shore seemed to fascinate the tall man, and for a time he did not speak.

Suddenly he concluded his minuet of horror. He wheeled about and faced the freckled man. He elaborately folded his arms.

"So," he said, in slow, formidable tones. "So! This all comes from your accursed vanity, your bathing-suit, your idiocy; you have murdered your best friend."

He turned away. His companion reeled as if stricken by an unexpected arm.

He stretched out his hands. "Tom, Tom," wailed he, beseechingly, "don't be such a fool."

The broad back of his friend was occupied by a contemptuous sneer.

Three ships fell off the horizon. Landward, the hues were blending. The whistle of a locomotive sounded from an infinite distance as if tooting in heaven.

"Tom! Tom! My dear boy," quavered the freckled man, "don't speak that way to me."

"Oh, no, of course not," said the other, still facing away and throwing the words over his shoulder. "You suppose I am going to accept all this calmly, don't you? Not make the slightest objection? Make no protest at all, hey?"

"Well, I—I——" began the freckled man.

The tall man's wrath suddenly exploded. "You've abducted me! That's the whole amount of it! You've abducted me!"

"I ain't," protested the freckled man. "You must think I'm a fool."

The tall man swore, and sitting down, dangled his legs angrily in the water. Natural law compelled his companion to occupy the other end of the raft.

Over the waters little shoals of fish spluttered, raising tiny tempests. Languid jelly-fish floated near, tremulously waving a thousand legs. A row of porpoises trundled along like a procession of cog-wheels. The sky became greyed save where over the land sunset colors were assembling.

The two voyagers, back to back and at either end of the raft, quarrelled at length.

"What did you want to follow me for?" demanded the freckled man in a voice of indignation.

"If your figure hadn't been so like a bottle, we wouldn't be here," replied the tall man.

CHAPTER III

THE fires in the west blazed away, and solemnity spread over the sea. Electric lights began to blink like eyes. Night menaced the voyagers with a dangerous darkness, and fear came to bind their souls together. They huddled fraternally in the middle of the raft.

"I feel like a molecule," said the freckled man in subdued tones.

"I'd give two dollars for a cigar," muttered the tall man.

A V-shaped flock of ducks flew towards Barnegat, between the voyagers and a remnant of yellow sky. Shadows and winds came from the vanished eastern horizon.

"I think I hear voices," said the freckled man.

"That Dollie Ramsdell was an awfully nice girl," said the tall man.

When the coldness of the sea night came to them, the freckled man found he could by a peculiar movement of his legs and arms encase himself in his bathing-dress. The tall man was compelled to whistle and shiver. As night settled finally over the sea, red and green lights began to dot the blackness. There were mysterious shadows between the waves.

"I see things comin'," murmured the freckled man.

"I wish I hadn't ordered that new dress-suit for the hop to-morrow night," said the tall man reflectively.

The sea became uneasy and heaved painfully, like a lost bosom, when little forgotten heart-bells try to chime with a pure sound. The voyagers cringed at magnified foam on distant wave crests. A moon came and looked at them.

"Somebody's here," whispered the freckled man.

"I wish I had an almanac," remarked the tall man, regarding the moon.

Presently they fell to staring at the red and green lights that twinkled about them.

"Providence will not leave us," asserted the freckled man.

"'Oh, we'll be picked up shortly. I owe money," said the tall man.

He began to thrum on an imaginary banjo.

"I have heard," said he, suddenly, "that captains with healthy ships beneath their feet will never turn back after having once started on a voyage. In that case we will be rescued by some ship bound for the golden seas of the south. Then, you'll be up to some of your confounded devilment, and we'll get put off. They'll maroon us! That's what they'll do! They'll maroon us! On an island with palm trees and sun-kissed maidens and all that. Sun-kissed maidens, eh? Great! They'd——"

He suddenly ceased and turned to stone. At a distance a great, green eye was contemplating the sea wanderers.

They stood up and did another dance. As they watched the eye grew larger.

Directly the form of a phantom-like ship came into view. About the great, green eye there bobbed small yellow dots. The wanderers could hear a far-away creaking of unseen tackle and flapping of shadowy sails. There came the melody of the waters as the ship's prow thrust its way.

The tall man delivered an oration.

"Ha!" he exclaimed, "here come our rescuers. The brave fellows! How I long to take the manly captain by the hand! You will soon see a white boat with a star on its bow drop from the side of yon ship. Kind sailors in blue and white will help us into the boat and conduct our wasted frames to the quarter-deck, where the handsome, bearded captain, with gold bands all around, will welcome us. Then in the hard-oak cabin, while the wine gurgles and the Havanas glow, we'll tell our tale of peril and privation."

The ship came on like a black hurrying animal with froth-filled maw. The two wanderers stood up and clasped hands.

Then they howled out a wild duet that rang over the wastes of sea.

The cries seemed to strike the ship.

Men with boots on yelled and ran about the deck. They picked up heavy articles and threw them down. They yelled more. After hideous creakings and flappings, the vessel stood still.

In the meantime the wanderers had been chanting their song for help. Out in the blackness they beckoned to the ship and coaxed.

A voice came to them.

"Hello," it said.

They puffed out their cheeks and began to shout. "Hello! Hello! Hello!"

"Wot do yeh want?" said the voice.

The two wanderers gazed at each other, and sat suddenly down on the raft. Some pall came sweeping over the sky and quenched their stars.

But almost immediately the tall man got up and brawled miscellaneous information. He stamped his foot, and frowning into the night, swore threateningly.

The vessel seemed fearful of these moaning voices that called from a hidden cavern of the water. And now one voice was filled with a menace. A number of men with enormous limbs that threw vast shadows over the sea as the lanterns flickered, held a debate and made gestures.

Off in the darkness, the tall man began to clamor like a mob. The freckled man sat in astounded silence, with his legs weak.

After a time one of the men of enormous limbs seized a

rope that was tugging at the stern and drew a small boat from the shadows. Three giants clambered in and rowed cautiously toward the raft. Silver water flashed in the gloom as the oars dipped.

About fifty feet from the raft the boat stopped. "Who er you?" asked a voice.

The tall man braced himself and explained. He drew vivid pictures, his twirling fingers illustrating like live brushes.

"Oh," said the three giants.

The voyagers deserted the raft. They looked back, feeling in their hearts a mite of tenderness for the wet planks. Later, they wriggled up the side of the vessel and climbed over the railing.

On deck they met a man.

He held a lantern to their faces. "Got any chewin' tewbacca?" he inquired.

"No," said the tall man, "we ain't."

The man had a bronze face and solitary whiskers. Peculiar lines about his mouth were shaped into an eternal smile of derision. His feet were bare, and clung handily to crevices.

Fearful trousers were supported by a piece of suspender that went up the wrong side of his chest and came down the right side of his back, dividing him into triangles.

"Ezekiel P. Sanford, capt'in, schooner 'Mary Jones,' of N'yack, N. Y., genelmen," he said.

"Ah!" said the tall man, "delighted, I'm sure."

There were a few moments of silence. The giants were hovering in the gloom and staring.

Suddenly astonishment exploded the captain.

"Wot th' devil——" he shouted. "Wot th' devil yeh got on?"

"Bathing-suits," said the tall man.

CHAPTER IV

THE schooner went on. The two voyagers sat down and watched. After a time they began to shiver. The soft blackness of the summer night passed away, and grey mists writhed over the sea. Soon lights of early dawn went changing across the sky, and the twin beacons on the highlands grew dim and sparkling faintly, as if a monster were dying. The dawn penetrated the marrow of the two men in bathing-dress.

The captain used to pause opposite them, hitch one hand in his suspender, and laugh.

"Well, I be dog-hanged," he frequently said.

The tall man grew furious. He snarled in a mad undertone to his companion. "This rescue ain't right. If I had known——"

He suddenly paused, transfixed by the captain's suspender. "It's goin' to break," cried he, in an ecstatic whisper. His eyes grew large with excitement as he watched the captain laugh. "It'll break in a minute, sure."

But the commander of the schooner recovered, and invited them to drink and eat. They followed him along the deck, and fell down a square black hole into the cabin.

It was a little den, with walls of a vanished whiteness. A lamp shed an orange light. In a sort of recess two little beds were hiding. A wooden table, immovable, as if the craft had been builded around it, sat in the middle of the floor. Overhead the square hole was studded with a dozen stars. A foot-worn ladder led to the heavens.

The captain produced ponderous crackers and some cold broiled ham. Then he vanished in the firmament like a fantastic comet.

The freckled man sat quite contentedly like a stout squaw in a blanket. The tall man walked about the cabin and sniffed. He was angered at the crudeness of the rescue, and his shrinking clothes made him feel too large. He contemplated his unhappy state.

Suddenly, he broke out. "I won't stand this, I tell you! Heavens and earth, look at the—say, what in the blazes did you want to get me in this thing for, anyhow? You're a fine old duffer, you are! Look at that ham!"

The freckled man grunted. He seemed somewhat blissful. He was seated upon a bench, comfortably enwrapped in his bathing-dress.

The tall man stormed about the cabin.

"This is an outrage! I'll see the captain! I'll tell him what I think of——"

He was interrupted by a pair of legs that appeared among the stars. The captain came down the ladder. He brought a coffee pot from the sky.

The tall man bristled forward. He was going to denounce everything.

The captain was intent upon the coffee pot, balancing it carefully, and leaving his unguided feet to find the steps of the ladder.

But the wrath of the tall man faded. He twirled his

fingers in excitement, and renewed his ecstatic whisperings to the freckled man.

"It's going to break! Look, quick, look! It'll break in a minute!"

He was transfixed with interest, forgetting his wrongs in staring at the perilous passage.

But the captain arrived on the floor with triumphant suspenders.

"Well," said he, "after yeh have eat, maybe ye'd like t'sleep some! If so, yeh can sleep on them beds."

The tall man made no reply, save in a strained undertone. "It'll break in about a minute! Look, Ted, look quick!"

The freckled man glanced in a little bed on which were heaped boots and oilskins. He made a courteous gesture.

"My dear sir, we could not think of depriving you of your beds. No, indeed. Just a couple of blankets if you have them, and we'll sleep very comfortable on these benches."

The captain protested, politely twisting his back and bobbing his head. The suspenders tugged and creaked. The tall man partially suppressed a cry, and took a step forward.

The freckled man was sleepily insistent, and shortly the captain gave over his deprecatory contortions. He fetched a pink quilt with yellow dots on it to the freckled man, and a black one with red roses on it to the tall man.

Again he vanished in the firmament. The tall man gazed until the last remnant of trousers disappeared from the sky. Then he wrapped himself up in his quilt and lay down. The freckled man was puffing contentedly, swathed like an infant. The yellow polka-dots rose and fell on the vast pink of his chest.

The wanderers slept. In the quiet could be heard the groanings of timbers as the sea seemed to crunch them together. The lapping of water along the vessel's side sounded like gaspings. An hundred spirits of the wind had got their wings entangled in the rigging, and, in soft voices, were pleading to be loosened.

The freckled man was awakened by a foreign noise. He opened his eyes and saw his companion standing by his couch.

His comrade's face was wan with suffering. His eyes glowed in the darkness. He raised his arms, spreading them out like a clergyman at a grave. He groaned deep in his chest.

"Good Lord!" yelled the freckled man, starting up. "Tom, Tom, what's th' matter?"

The tall man spoke in a fearful voice. "To New York," he said, "to New York in our bathing-suits."

The freckled man sank back. The shadows of the cabin threw mysteries about the figure of the tall man, arrayed like some ancient and potent astrologer in the black quilt with the red roses on it.

CHAPTER V

DIRECTLY the tall man went and lay down and began to groan.

The freckled man felt the miseries of the world upon him. He grew angry at the tall man awakening him. They quarrelled.

"Well," said the tall man, finally, "we're in a fix."

"I know that," said the other, sharply.

They regarded the ceiling in silence.

"What in the thunder are we going to do?" demanded the tall man, after a time. His companion was still silent. "Say," repeated he, angrily, "what in the thunder are we going to do?"

"I'm sure I don't know," said the freckled man in a dismal voice.

"Well, think of something," roared the other. "Think of something, you old fool. You don't want to make any more idiots of yourself, do you?"

"I ain't made an idiot of myself."

"Well, think. Know anybody in the city?"

"I know a fellow up in Harlem," said the freckled man.

"You know a fellow up in Harlem," howled the tall man. "Up in Harlem! How the dickens are we to—say, you're crazy!"

"We can take a cab," cried the other, waxing indignant.

The tall man grew suddenly calm. "Do you know any one else?" he asked, measuredly.

"I know another fellow somewhere on Park Place."

"Somewhere on Park Place," repeated the tall man in an unnatural manner. "Somewhere on Park Place." With an air of sublime resignation he turned his face to the wall.

The freckled man sat erect and frowned in the direction of his companion. "Well, now, I suppose you are going to sulk. You make me ill! It's the best we can do, ain't it? Hire a cab and go look that fellow up on Park—— What's that? You can't afford it? What nonsense! You are getting——

Oh! Well, maybe we can beg some clothes of the captain. Eh? Did I see 'im? Certainly, I saw 'im. Yes, it is improbable that a man who wears trousers like that can have clothes to lend. No, I won't wear oilskins and a sou'-wester. To Athens? Of course not! I don't know where it is. Do you? I thought not. With all your grumbling about other people, you never know anything important yourself. What? Broadway? I'll be hanged first. We can get off at Harlem, man alive. There are no cabs in Harlem. I don't think we can bribe a sailor to take us ashore and bring a cab to the dock, for the very simple reason that we have nothing to bribe him with. What? No, of course not. See here, Tom Sharp, don't you swear at me like that. I won't have it. What's that? I ain't, either. I ain't. What? I am not. It's no such thing. I ain't. I've got more than you have, anyway. Well, you ain't doing anything so very brilliant yourself—just lying there and cussin'." At length the tall man feigned prodigiously to snore. The freckled man thought with such vigor that he fell asleep.

After a time he dreamed that he was in a forest where bass drums grew on trees. There came a strong wind that banged the fruit about like empty pods. A frightful din was in his ears.

He awoke to find the captain of the schooner standing over him.

"We're at New York now," said the captain, raising his voice above the thumping and banging that was being done on deck, "an' I s'pose you fellers wanta go ashore." He chuckled in an exasperating manner. "Jes' sing out when yeh wanta go," he added, leering at the freckled man.

The tall man awoke, came over and grasped the captain by the throat.

"If you laugh again I'll kill you," he said.

The captain gurgled and waved his legs and arms.

"In the first place," the tall man continued, "you rescued us in a deucedly shabby manner. It makes me ill to think of it. I've a mind to mop you 'round just for that. In the second place, your vessel is bound for Athens, N. Y., and there's no sense in it. Now, will you or will you not turn this ship about and take us back where our clothes are, or to Philadelphia, where we belong?"

He furiously shook the captain. Then he eased his grip and awaited a reply.

"I can't," yelled the captain, "I can't. This vessel don't belong to me. I've got to——"

"Well, then," interrupted the tall man, "can you lend us some clothes?"

"Hain't got none," replied the captain, promptly. His face was red, and his eyes were glaring.

"Well, then," said the tall man, "can you lend us some money?"

"Hain't got none," replied the captain, promptly. Something overcame him and he laughed.

"Thunderation," roared the tall man. He seized the captain, who began to have wriggling contortions. The tall man kneaded him as if he were biscuits. "You infernal scoundrel," he bellowed, "this whole affair is some wretched plot, and you are in it. I am about to kill you."

The solitary whisker of the captain did acrobatic feats like a strange demon upon his chin. His eyes stood perilously from his head. The suspender wheezed and tugged like the tackle of a sail.

Suddenly the tall man released his hold. Great expectancy sat upon his features. "It's going to break!" he cried, rubbing his hands.

But the captain howled and vanished in the sky.

The freckled man then came forward. He appeared filled with sarcasm.

"So!" said he. "So, you've settled the matter. The captain is the only man in the world who can help us, and I daresay he'll do anything he can now."

"That's all right," said the tall man. "If you don't like the way I run things you shouldn't have come on this trip at all."

They had another quarrel.

At the end of it they went on deck. The captain stood at the stern addressing the bow with opprobrious language. When he perceived the voyagers he began to fling his fists about in the air.

"I'm goin' to put yeh off!" he yelled. The wanderers stared at each other.

"Hum," said the tall man.

The freckled man looked at his companion. "He's going to put us off, you see," he said, complacently.

The tall man began to walk about and move his shoulders. "I'd like to see you do it," he said, defiantly.

The captain tugged at a rope. A boat came at his bidding.

"I'd like to see you do it," the tall man repeated, continually. An imperturbable man in rubber boots climbed down in the boat and seized the oars. The captain motioned downward. His whisker had a triumphant appearance.

The two wanderers looked at the boat. "I guess we'll have to get in," murmured the freckled man.

The tall man was standing like a granite column. "I won't," said he. "I won't! I don't care what you do, but I won't!"

"Well, but——" expostulated the other. They held a furious debate.

In the meantime the captain was darting about making sinister gestures, but the back of the tall man held him at bay. The crew, much depleted by the departure of the imperturbable man into the boat, looked on from the bow.

"You're a fool," the freckled man concluded his argument.

"So?" inquired the tall man, highly exasperated.

"So! Well, if you think you're so bright, we'll go in the boat, and then you'll see."

He climbed down into the craft and seated himself in an ominous manner at the stern.

"You'll see," he said to his companion, as the latter floundered heavily down. "You'll see!"

The man in rubber boots calmly rowed the boat toward the shore. As they went, the captain leaned over the railing and laughed. The freckled man was seated very victoriously.

"Well, wasn't this the right thing after all?" he inquired in a pleasant voice. The tall man made no reply.

CHAPTER VI

As they neared the dock something seemed suddenly to occur to the freckled man.

"Great heavens!" he murmured. He stared at the approaching shore.

"My, what a plight, Tommy!" he quavered.

"Do you think so?" spoke up the tall man. "Why, I really thought you liked it." He laughed in a hard voice. "Lord, what a figure you'll cut."

This laugh jarred the freckled man's soul. He became mad.

"Thunderation, turn the boat around!" he roared. "Turn 'er round, quick! Man alive, we can't—turn 'er round, d'ye hear!"

The tall man in the stern gazed at his companion with glowing eyes.

"Certainly not," he said. "We're going on. You insisted upon it." He began to prod his companion with words.

The freckled man stood up and waved his arms.

"Sit down," said the tall man. "You'll tip the boat over."

The other man began to shout.

"Sit down!" said the tall man again.

Words bubbled from the freckled man's mouth. There was a little torrent of sentences that almost choked him. And he protested passionately with his hands.

But the boat went on to the shadow of the docks. The tall man was intent upon balancing it as it rocked dangerously during his comrade's oration.

"Sit down," he continually repeated.

"I won't," raged the freckled man. "I won't do anything." The boat wobbled with these words.

"Say," he continued, addressing the oarsman, "just turn this boat round, will you? Where in the thunder are you taking us to, anyhow?"

The oarsman looked at the sky and thought. Finally he spoke. "I'm doin' what the cap'n sed."

"Well, what in th' blazes do I care what the cap'n sed?" demanded the freckled man. He took a violent step. "You just turn this round or——"

The small craft reeled. Over one side water came flashing in. The freckled man cried out in fear, and gave a jump to the other side. The tall man roared orders, and the oarsman made efforts. The boat acted for a moment like an animal on a slackened wire. Then it upset.

"Sit down!" said the tall man, in a final roar as he was plunged into the water. The oarsman dropped his oars to grapple with the gunwale. He went down saying unknown words. The freckled man's explanation or apology was strangled by the water.

Two or three tugs let off whistles of astonishment, and continued on their paths. A man dozing on a dock aroused and began to caper. The passengers on a ferry-boat all ran to the near railing.

A miraculous person in a small boat was bobbing on the waves near the piers. He sculled hastily toward the scene. It was a swirl of waters in the midst of which the dark bottom of the boat appeared, whale-like.

Two heads suddenly came up.

"839," said the freckled man, chokingly. "That's it! 839!"

"What is?" said the tall man.

"That's the number of that feller on Park Place. I just remembered."

"You're the bloomingest——" the tall man said.

"It wasn't my fault," interrupted his companion. "If you hadn't——" He tried to gesticulate, but one hand held to the keel of the boat, and the other was supporting the form of the oarsman. The latter had fought a battle with his immense rubber boots and had been conquered.

The rescuer in the other small boat came fiercely. As his craft glided up, he reached out and grasped the tall man by the collar and dragged him into the boat, interrupting what was, under the circumstances, a very brilliant flow of rhetoric directed at the freckled man. The oarsman of the wrecked craft was taken tenderly over the gunwale and laid in the bottom of the boat. Puffing and blowing, the freckled man climbed in.

"You'll upset this one before we can get ashore," the other voyager remarked.

As they turned toward the land they saw that the nearest dock was lined with people. The freckled man gave a little moan.

But the staring eyes of the crowd were fixed on the limp form of the man in rubber boots. A hundred hands reached down to help lift the body up. On the dock some men grabbed it and began to beat it and roll it. A policeman tossed the spectators about. Each individual in the heaving crowd sought to fasten his eyes on the blue-tinted face of the man in the rubber boots. They surged to and fro, while the policeman beat them indiscriminately.

The wanderers came modestly up the dock and gazed shrinkingly at the throng. They stood for a moment, holding their breath to see the first finger of amazement levelled at them.

But the crowd bended and surged in absorbing anxiety to view the man in rubber boots, whose face fascinated them. The sea-wanderers were as though they were not there.

They stood without the jam and whispered hurriedly.

"839," said the freckled man.

"All right," said the tall man.

Under the pommeling hands the oarsman showed signs of life. The voyagers watched him make a protesting kick at the leg of the crowd, the while uttering angry groans.

"He's better," said the tall man, softly; "let's make off."

Together they stole noiselessly up the dock. Directly in front of it they found a row of six cabs.

The drivers on top were filled with a mighty curiosity. They had driven hurriedly from the adjacent ferry-house when they had seen the first running sign of an accident. They were straining on their toes and gazing at the tossing backs of the men in the crowd.

The wanderers made a little detour, and then went rapidly towards a cab. They stopped in front of it and looked up.

"Driver," called the tall man, softly.

The man was intent.

"Driver," breathed the freckled man. They stood for a moment and gazed imploringly.

The cabman suddenly moved his feet. "By Jimmy, I bet he's a gonner," he said, in an ecstacy, and he again relapsed into a statue.

The freckled man groaned and wrung his hands. The tall man climbed into the cab.

"Come in here," he said to his companion. The freckled man climbed in, and the tall man reached over and pulled the door shut. Then he put his head out the window.

"Driver," he roared, sternly, "839 Park Place—and quick."

The driver looked down and met the eye of the tall man. "Eh?—Oh—839? Park Place? Yessir." He reluctantly gave his horse a clump on the back. As the conveyance rattled off the wanderers huddled back among the dingy cushions and heaved great breaths of relief.

"Well, it's all over," said the freckled man, finally. "We're about out of it. And quicker than I expected. Much quicker. It looked to me sometimes that we were doomed. I am thankful to find it not so. I am rejoiced. And I hope and trust that you—well, I don't wish to—perhaps it is not the proper time to—that is, I don't wish to intrude a moral at an inopportune moment, but, my dear, dear fellow, I think the time is ripe to point out to you that your obstinacy, your selfishness, your villainous temper, and your various other faults can make it just as unpleasant for your own-self, my dear boy, as they frequently do for other people. You can see what you brought us to, and I most sincerely hope, my dear, dear fellow, that I shall soon see those signs in you which shall lead me to believe that you have become a wiser man."

THE END OF THE BATTLE

THE END OF THE BATTLE

A SERGEANT, a corporal, and fourteen men of the Twelfth Regiment of the Line had been sent out to occupy a house on the main highway. They would be at least a half of a mile in advance of any other picket of their own people. Sergeant Morton was deeply angry at being sent on this duty. He said that he was over-worked. There were at least two sergeants, he claimed furiously, whose turn it should have been to go on this arduous mission. He was treated unfairly; he was abused by his superiors; why did any damned fool ever join the army? As for him he would get out of it as soon as possible; he was sick of it; the life of a dog. All this he said to the corporal, who listened attentively, giving grunts of respectful assent. On the way to this post two privates took occasion to drop to the rear and pilfer in the orchard of a deserted plantation. When the sergeant discovered this absence, he grew black with a rage which was an accumulation of all his irritations. "Run, you!" he howled. "Bring them here! I'll show them——" A private ran swiftly to the rear. The remainder of the squad began to shout nervously at the two delinquents, whose figures they could see in the deep shade of the orchard, hurriedly picking fruit from the ground and cramming it within their shirts, next to their skins. The beseeching cries

of their comrades stirred the criminals more than did the
barking of the sergeant. They ran to rejoin the squad, while
holding their loaded bosoms and with their mouths open with
aggrieved explanations.

Jones faced the sergeant with a horrible cancer marked in
bumps on his left side. The disease of Patterson showed
quite around the front of his waist in many protuberances.
"A nice pair!" said the sergeant, with sudden frigidity.
"You're the kind of soldiers a man wants to choose for a
dangerous outpost duty, ain't you?"

The two privates stood at attention, still looking much aggrieved. "We only——" began Jones huskily.

"Oh, you 'only!'" cried the sergeant. "Yes, you 'only.'
I know all about that. But if you think you are going to
trifle with me——"

A moment later the squad moved on towards its station.
Behind the sergeant's back Jones and Patterson were slyly
passing apples and pears to their friends while the sergeant
expounded eloquently to the corporal. "You see what kind
of men are in the army now. Why, when I joined the regiment it was a very different thing, I can tell you. Then a
sergeant had some authority, and if a man disobeyed orders,
he had a very small chance of escaping something extremely
serious. But now! Good God! If I report these men, the
captain will look over a lot of beastly orderly sheets and
say—'Haw, eh, well, Sergeant Morton, these men seem to
have very good records; very good records, indeed. I can't
be too hard on them; no, not too hard.'" Continued the
sergeant: "I tell you, Flagler, the army is no place for a
decent man."

Flagler, the corporal, answered with a sincerity of appreciation which with him had become a science. "I think you are right, sergeant," he answered.

Behind them the privates mumbled discreetly. "Damn this sergeant of ours. He thinks we are made of wood. I don't see any reason for all this strictness when we are on active service. It isn't like being at home in barracks! There is no great harm in a couple of men dropping out to raid an orchard of the enemy when all the world knows that we haven't had a decent meal in twenty days."

The reddened face of Sergeant Morton suddenly showed to the rear. "A little more marching and less talking," he said.

When he came to the house he had been ordered to occupy the sergeant sniffed with disdain. "These people must have lived like cattle," he said angrily. To be sure, the place was not alluring. The ground floor had been used for the housing of cattle, and it was dark and terrible. A flight of steps led to the lofty first floor, which was denuded but respectable. The sergeant's visage lightened when he saw the strong walls of stone and cement. "Unless they turn guns on us, they will never get us out of here," he said cheerfully to the squad. The men, anxious to keep him in an amiable mood, all hurriedly grinned and seemed very appreciative and pleased. "I'll make this into a fortress," he announced. He sent Jones and Patterson, the two orchard thieves, out on sentry-duty. He worked the others, then, until he could think of no more things to tell them to do. Afterwards he went forth, with a major-general's serious scowl, and examined the ground in front of his position. In returning he came upon a sentry, Jones, munching an apple. He sternly commanded him to throw it away.

The men spread their blankets on the floors of the bare rooms, and putting their packs under their heads and lighting their pipes, they lived an easy peace. Bees hummed in the garden, and a scent of flowers came through the open window. A great fan-shaped bit of sunshine smote the face of one man, and he indolently cursed as he moved his primitive bed to a shadier place.

Another private explained to a comrade: "This is all nonsense anyhow. No sense in occupying this post. They——"

"But, of course," said the corporal, "when she told me herself that she cared more for me than she did for him, I wasn't going to stand any of his talk——" The corporal's listener was so sleepy that he could only grunt his sympathy.

There was a sudden little spatter of shooting. A cry from Jones rang out. With no intermediate scrambling, the sergeant leaped straight to his feet. "Now," he cried, "let us see what you are made of! If," he added bitterly, "you are made of anything!"

A man yelled: "Good God, can't you see you're all tangled up in my cartridge belt?"

Another man yelled: "Keep off my legs! Can't you walk on the floor?"

To the windows there was a blind rush of slumberous men, who brushed hair from their eyes even as they made ready their rifles. Jones and Patterson came stumbling up the steps, crying dreadful information. Already the enemy's bullets were spitting and singing over the house.

The sergeant suddenly was stiff and cold with a sense of the importance of the thing. "Wait until you see one," he drawled loudly and calmly, "then shoot."

For some moments the enemy's bullets swung swifter than lightning over the house without anybody being able to discover a target. In this interval a man was shot in the throat. He gurgled, and then lay down on the floor. The blood slowly waved down the brown skin of his neck while he looked meekly at his comrades.

There was a howl. "There they are! There they come!" The rifles crackled. A light smoke drifted idly through the rooms. There was a strong odor as if from burnt paper and the powder of firecrackers. The men were silent. Through the windows and about the house the bullets of an entirely invisible enemy moaned, hummed, spat, burst, and sang.

The men began to curse. "Why can't we see them?" they muttered through their teeth. The sergeant was still frigid. He answered soothingly as if he were directly reprehensible for this behavior of the enemy. "Wait a moment. You will soon be able to see them. There! Give it to them!" A little skirt of black figures had appeared in a field. It was really like shooting at an upright needle from the full length of a ballroom. But the men's spirits improved as soon as the enemy—this mysterious enemy—became a tangible thing, and far off. They had believed the foe to be shooting at them from the adjacent garden.

"Now," said the sergeant ambitiously, "we can beat them off easily if you men are good enough."

A man called out in a tone of quick, great interest. "See

that fellow on horseback, Bill? Isn't he on horseback? I thought he was on horseback."

There was a fusilade against another side of the house. The sergeant dashed into the room which commanded the situation. He found a dead soldier on the floor. He rushed out howling: "When was Knowles killed? When was Knowles killed? When was Knowles killed? Damn it, when was Knowles killed?" It was absolutely essential to find out the exact moment this man died. A blackened private turned upon his sergeant and demanded: "How in hell do I know?" Sergeant Morton had a sense of anger so brief that in the next second he cried: "Patterson!" He had even forgotten his vital interest in the time of Knowles' death.

"Yes?" said Patterson, his face set with some deep-rooted quality of determination. Still, he was a mere farm boy.

"Go in to Knowles' window and shoot at those people," said the sergeant hoarsely. Afterwards he coughed. Some of the fumes of the fight had made way to his lungs.

Patterson looked at the door into this other room. He looked at it as if he suspected it was to be his death-chamber. Then he entered and stood across the body of Knowles and fired vigorously into a group of plum trees.

"They can't take this house," declared the sergeant in a contemptuous and argumentative tone. He was apparently replying to somebody. The man who had been shot in the throat looked up at him. Eight men were firing from the windows. The sergeant detected in a corner three wounded men talking together feebly. "Don't you think there is anything to do?" he bawled. 'Go and get Knowles' cartridges and give them to somebody who can use them! Take Simpson's too." The man who had been shot in the throat looked at him. Of the three wounded men who had been talking, one said: "My leg is all doubled up under me, sergeant." He spoke apologetically.

Meantime the sergeant was re-loading his rifle. His foot slipped in the blood of the man who had been shot in the throat, and the military boot made a greasy red streak on the floor.

"Why, we can hold this place!" shouted the sergeant jubilantly. "Who says we can't?"

Corporal Flagler suddenly spun away from his window and fell in a heap.

"Sergeant," murmured a man as he dropped to a seat on the floor out of danger, "I can't stand this. I swear I can't. I think we should run away."

Morton, with the kindly eyes of a good shepherd, looked at the man. "You are afraid, Johnston, you are afraid," he said softly. The man struggled to his feet, cast upon the sergeant a gaze full of admiration, reproach, and despair, and returned to his post. A moment later he pitched forward, and thereafter his body hung out of the window, his arms straight and the fists clenched. Incidentally this corpse was pierced afterwards by chance three times by bullets of the enemy.

The sergeant laid his rifle against the stonework of the window-frame and shot with care until his magazine was empty. Behind him a man, simply grazed on the elbow, was wildly sobbing like a girl. "Damn it, shut up!" said Morton, without turning his head. Before him was a vista of a garden, fields, clumps of trees, woods, populated at the time with little fleeting figures.

He grew furious. "Why didn't he send me orders?" he cried aloud. The emphasis on the word "he" was impressive. A mile back on the road a galloper of the Hussars lay dead beside his dead horse.

The man who had been grazed on the elbow still set up his bleat. Morton's fury veered to this soldier. "Can't you shut up? Can't you shut up? Can't you shut up? Fight! That's the thing to do. Fight!"

A bullet struck Morton, and he fell upon the man who had been shot in the throat. There was a sickening moment. Then the sergeant rolled off to a position upon the bloody floor. He turned himself with a last effort until he could look at the wounded who were able to look at him.

"Kim up, the Kickers," he said thickly. His arms weakened and he dropped on his face.

After an interval a young subaltern of the enemy's infantry, followed by his eager men, burst into this reeking interior. But just over the threshold he halted before the scene of blood and death. He turned with a shrug to his sergeant. "God, I should have estimated them at least one hundred strong."

THE UPTURNED FACE

THE UPTURNED FACE

"WHAT will we do now?" said the adjutant, troubled and excited.

"Bury him," said Timothy Lean.

The two officers looked down close to their toes where lay the body of their comrade. The face was chalk-blue; gleaming eyes stared at the sky. Over the two upright figures was a windy sound of bullets, and on the top of the hill Lean's prostrate company of Spitzbergen infantry was firing measured volleys.

"Don't you think it would be better——" began the adjutant. "We might leave him until to-morrow."

"No," said Lean. "I can't hold that post an hour longer. I've got to fall back, and we've got to bury old Bill."

"Of course," said the adjutant, at once. "Your men got intrenching tools?"

Lean shouted back to his little line, and two men came slowly, one with a pick, one with a shovel. They started in the direction of the Rostina sharp-shooters. Bullets cracked near their ears. "Dig here," said Lean gruffly. The men, thus caused to lower their glances to the turf, became hurried and frightened merely because they could not look to see whence the bullets came. The dull beat of the pick

striking the earth sounded amid the swift snap of close bullets. Presently the other private began to shovel.

"I suppose," said the adjutant, slowly, "we'd better search
his clothes for—things."

Lean nodded. Together in curious abstraction they looked
at the body. Then Lean stirred his shoulders suddenly, arous-
ing himself.

"Yes," he said, "we'd better see what he's got." He
dropped to his knees, and his hands approached the body of
the dead officer. But his hands wavered over the buttons
of the tunic. The first button was brick-red with drying
blood, and he did not seem to dare touch it.

"Go on," said the adjutant, hoarsely.

Lean stretched his wooden hand, and his fingers fumbled
the blood-stained buttons. At last he rose with ghastly face.
He had gathered a watch, a whistle, a pipe, a tobacco pouch,
a handkerchief, a little case of cards and papers. He looked
at the adjutant. There was a silence. The adjutant was
feeling that he had been a coward to make Lean do all the
grisly business.

"Well," said Lean, "that's all, I think. You have his
sword and revolver?"

"Yes," said the adjutant, his face working, and then he
burst out in a sudden strange fury at the two privates. "Why
don't you hurry up with that grave? What are you doing,
anyhow? Hurry, do you hear? I never saw such stupid——"

Even as he cried out in his passion the two men were
laboring for their lives. Ever overhead the bullets were
spitting.

The grave was finished. It was not a masterpiece—a poor little shallow thing. Lean and the adjutant again looked at each other in a curious silent communication.

Suddenly the adjutant croaked out a weird laugh. It was a terrible laugh, which had its origin in that part of the mind which is first moved by the singing of the nerves. "Well," he said, humorously to Lean, "I suppose we had best tumble him in."

"Yes," said Lean. The two privates stood waiting, bent over their implements. "I suppose," said Lean, "it would be better if we laid him in ourselves."

"Yes," said the adjutant. Then apparently remembering that he had made Lean search the body, he stooped with great fortitude and took hold of the dead officer's clothing. Lean joined him. Both were particular that their fingers should not feel the corpse. They tugged away; the corpse lifted, heaved, toppled, flopped into the grave, and the two officers, straightening, looked again at each other—they were always looking at each other. They sighed with relief.

The adjutant said, "I suppose we should—we should say something. Do you know the service, Tim?"

"They don't read the service until the grave is filled in," said Lean, pressing his lips to an academic expression.

"Don't they?" said the adjutant, shocked that he had made the mistake.

"Oh, well," he cried, suddenly, "let us—let us say something—while he can hear us."

"All right," said Lean. "Do you know the service?"

"I can't remember a line of it," said the adjutant.

Lean was extremely dubious. "I can repeat two lines, but——"

"Well, do it," said the adjutant. "Go as far as you can. That's better than nothing. And the beasts have got our range exactly."

Lean looked at his two men. "Attention," he barked. The privates came to attention with a click, looking much aggrieved. The adjutant lowered his helmet to his knee. Lean, bareheaded, he stood over the grave. The Rostina sharpshooters fired briskly.

"Oh, Father, our friend has sunk in the deep waters of death, but his spirit has leaped toward Thee as the bubble arises from the lips of the drowning. Perceive, we beseech, O Father, the little flying bubble, and——"

Lean, although husky and ashamed, had suffered no hesitation up to this point, but he stopped with a hopeless feeling and looked at the corpse.

The adjutant moved uneasily. "And from Thy superb heights——" he began, and then he too came to an end.

"And from Thy superb heights," said Lean.

The adjutant suddenly remembered a phrase in the back part of the Spitzbergen burial service, and he exploited it with the triumphant manner of a man who has recalled everything, and can go on.

"Oh, God, have mercy——"

"Oh, God, have mercy——" said Lean.

"Mercy," repeated the adjutant, in quick failure.

"Mercy," said Lean. And then he was moved by some violence of feeling, for he turned suddenly upon his two men and tigerishly said, "Throw the dirt in."

The fire of the Rostina sharpshooters was accurate and continuous.

*   *   *   *   *   *   *

One of the aggrieved privates came forward with his shovel. He lifted his first shovel-load of earth, and for a moment of inexplicable hesitation it was held poised above this corpse, which from its chalk-blue face looked keenly out from the grave. Then the soldier emptied his shovel on—on the feet.

Timothy Lean felt as if tons had been swiftly lifted from off his forehead. He had felt that perhaps the private might empty the shovel on—on the face. It had been emptied on the feet. There was a great point gained there—ha, ha!— the first shovelful had been emptied on the feet. How satisfactory!

The adjutant began to babble. "Well, of course—a man we've messed with all these years—impossible—you can't, you know, leave your intimate friends rotting on the field. Go on, for God's sake, and shovel, you!"

The man with the shovel suddenly ducked, grabbed his left arm with his right hand, and looked at his officer for orders. Lean picked the shovel from the ground. "Go to the rear," he said to the wounded man. He also addressed the other private. "You get under cover, too; I'll finish this business."

The wounded man scrambled hard still for the top of the ridge without devoting any glances to the direction whence the bullets came, and the other man followed at an equal pace; but he was different, in that he looked back anxiously three times.

This is merely the way—often—of the hit and unhit.

Timothy Lean filled the shovel, hesitated, and then in a movement which was like a gesture of abhorrence he flung the dirt into the grave, and as it landed it made a sound—plop! Lean suddenly stopped and mopped his brow—a tired laborer.

"Perhaps we have been wrong," said the adjutant. His glance wavered stupidly. "It might have been better if we hadn't buried him just at this time. Of course, if we advance to-morrow the body would have been——"

"Damn you," said Lean, "shut your mouth!" He was not the senior officer.

He again filled the shovel and flung the earth. Always the earth made that sound—plop! For a space Lean worked frantically, like a man digging himself out of danger.

Soon there was nothing to be seen but the chalk-blue face. Lean filled the shovel. "Good God," he cried to the adjutant. "Why didn't you turn him somehow when you put him in? This——" Then Lean began to stutter.

The adjutant understood. He was pale to the lips. "Go on, man," he cried, beseechingly, almost in a shout. Lean swung back the shovel. It went forward in a pendulum curve. When the earth landed it made a sound—plop!

AN EPISODE OF WAR

AN EPISODE OF WAR

THE lieutenant's rubber blanket lay on the ground, and upon it he had poured the company's supply of coffee. Corporals and other representatives of the grimy and hot-throated men who lined the breastwork had come for each squad's portion.

The lieutenant was frowning and serious at this task of division. His lips pursed as he drew with his sword various crevices in the heap until brown squares of coffee, astoundingly equal in size, appeared on the blanket. He was on the verge of a great triumph in mathematics, and the corporals were thronging forward, each to reap a little square, when suddenly the lieutenant cried out and looked quickly at a man near him as if he suspected it was a case of personal assault. The others cried out also when they saw blood upon the lieutenant's sleeve.

He had winced like a man stung, swayed dangerously, and then straightened. The sound of his hoarse breathing was plainly audible. He looked sadly, mystically, over the breastwork at the green face of a wood, where now were many little puffs of white smoke. During this moment the men about him gazed statue-like and silent, astonished and awed by this catastrophe which happened when catastrophes were not expected—when they had leisure to observe it.

As the lieutenant stared at the wood, they too swung their

heads, so that for another instant all hands, still silent, contemplated the distant forest as if their minds were fixed upon the mystery of a bullet's journey.

The officer had, of course, been compelled to take his sword into his left hand. He did not hold it by the hilt. He gripped it at the middle of the blade, awkwardly. Turning his eyes from the hostile wood, he looked at the sword as he held it there, and seemed puzzled as to what to do with it, where to put it. In short, this weapon had of a sudden become a strange thing to him. He looked at it in a kind of stupefaction, as if he had been endowed with a trident, a sceptre, or a spade.

Finally he tried to sheath it. To sheath a sword held by the left hand, at the middle of the blade, in a scabbard hung at the left hip, is a feat worthy of a sawdust ring. This wounded officer engaged in a desperate struggle with the sword and the wobbling scabbard, and during the time of it he breathed like a wrestler.

But at this instant the men, the spectators, awoke from their stone-like poses and crowded forward sympathetically. The orderly-sergeant took the sword and tenderly placed it in the scabbard. At the time, he leaned nervously backward, and did not allow even his finger to brush the body of the lieutenant. A wound gives strange dignity to him who bears it. Well men shy from this new and terrible majesty. It is as if the wounded man's hand is upon the curtain which hangs before the revelations of all existence—the meaning of ants, potentates, wars, cities, sunshine, snow, a feather dropped from a bird's wing; and the power of it sheds radiance upon a bloody form, and makes the other men under-

stand sometimes that they are little. His comrades look at
him with large eyes thoughtfully. Moreover, they fear
vaguely that the weight of a finger upon him might send him
headlong, precipitate the tragedy, hurl him at once into the
dim, grey unknown. And so the orderly-sergeant, while
sheathing the sword, leaned nervously backward.

There were others who proffered assistance. One timidly
presented his shoulder and asked the lieutenant if he cared
to lean upon it, but the latter waved him away mournfully.
He wore the look of one who knows he is the victim of a
terrible disease and understands his helplessness. He again
stared over the breastwork at the forest, and then turning
went slowly rearward. He held his right wrist tenderly in
his left hand as if the wounded arm was made of very brittle
glass.

And the men in silence stared at the wood, then at the
departing lieutenant—then at the wood, then at the lieutenant.

As the wounded officer passed from the line of battle, he
was enabled to see many things which as a participant in the
fight were unknown to him. He saw a general on a black
horse gazing over the lines of blue infantry at the green
woods which veiled his problems. An aide galloped furiously, dragged his horse suddenly to a halt, saluted, and presented a paper. It was, for a wonder, precisely like an his-
torical painting.

To the rear of the general and his staff a group, composed
of a bugler, two or three orderlies, and the bearer of the
corps standard, all upon maniacal horses, were working like
slaves to hold their ground, preserve their respectful inter-

val, while the shells boomed in the air about them, and caused their chargers to make furious quivering leaps.

A battery, a tumultuous and shining mass, was swirling toward the right. The wild thud of hoofs, the cries of the riders shouting blame and praise, menace and encouragement, and, last the roar of the wheels, the slant of the glistening guns, brought the lieutenant to an intent pause. The battery swept in curves that stirred the heart; it made halts as dramatic as the crash of a wave on the rocks, and when it fled onward, this aggregation of wheels, levers, motors, had a beautiful unity, as if it were a missile. The sound of it was a war-chorus that reached into the depths of man's emotion.

The lieutenant, still holding his arm as if it were of glass, stood watching this battery until all detail of it was lost, save the figures of the riders, which rose and fell and waved lashes over the black mass.

Later, he turned his eyes toward the battle where the shooting sometimes crackled like bush-fires, sometimes sputtered with exasperating irregularity, and sometimes reverberated like the thunder. He saw the smoke rolling upward and saw crowds of men who ran and cheered, or stood and blazed away at the inscrutable distance.

He came upon some stragglers, and they told him how to find the field hospital. They described its exact location. In fact, these men, no longer having part in the battle, knew more of it than others. They told the performance of every corps, every division, the opinion of every general. The lieutenant, carrying his wounded arm rearward, looked upon them with wonder.

At the roadside a brigade was making coffee and buzzing with talk like a girls' boarding-school. Several officers came out to him and inquired concerning things of which he knew nothing. One, seeing his arm, began to scold. "Why, man, that's no way to do. You want to fix that thing." He appropriated the lieutenant and the lieutenant's wound. He cut the sleeve and laid bare the arm, every nerve of which softly fluttered under his touch. He bound his handkerchief over the wound, scolding away in the meantime. His tone allowed one to think that he was in the habit of being wounded every day. The lieutenant hung his head, feeling, in this presence, that he did not know how to be correctly wounded.

The low white tents of the hospital were grouped around an old school-house. There was here a singular commotion. In the foreground two ambulances interlocked wheels in the deep mud. The drivers were tossing the blame of it back and forth, gesticulating and berating, while from the ambulances, both crammed with wounded, there came an occasional groan. An interminable crowd of bandaged men were coming and going. Great numbers sat under the trees nursing heads or arms or legs. There was a dispute of some kind raging on the steps of the school-house. Sitting with his back against a tree a man with a face as grey as a new army blanket was serenely smoking a corn-cob pipe. The lieutenant wished to rush forward and inform him that he was dying.

A busy surgeon was passing near the lieutenant. "Good-morning," he said, with a friendly smile. Then he caught sight of the lieutenant's arm and his face at once changed.

"Well, let's have a look at it." He seemed possessed suddenly of a great contempt for the lieutenant. This wound evidently placed the latter on a very low social plane. The doctor cried out impatiently, "What mutton-head had tied it up that way anyhow?" The lieutenant answered, "Oh, a man."

When the wound was disclosed the doctor fingered it disdainfully. "Humph," he said. "You come along with me and I'll 'tend to you." His voice contained the same scorn as if he were saying, "You will have to go to jail."

The lieutenant had been very meek, but now his face flushed, and he looked into the doctor's eyes. "I guess I won't have it amputated," he said.

"Nonsense, man! Nonsense! Nonsense!" cried the doctor. "Come along, now. I won't amputate it. Come along. Don't be a baby."

"Let go of me," said the lieutenant, holding back wrathfully, his glance fixed upon the door of the old school-house, as sinister to him as the portals of death.

And this is the story of how the lieutenant lost his arm. When he reached home, his sisters, his mother, his wife, sobbed for a long time at the sight of the flat sleeve. "Oh, well," he said, standing shamefaced amid these tears, "I don't suppose it matters so much as all that."

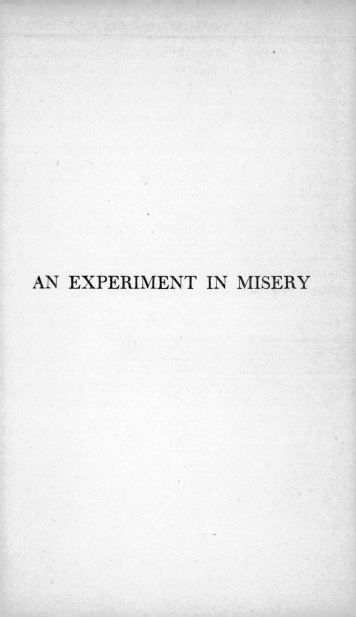

AN EXPERIMENT IN MISERY

AN EXPERIMENT IN MISERY

I⊤ was late at night, and a fine rain was swirling softly down, causing the pavements to glisten with hue of steel and blue and yellow in the rays of the innumerable lights. A youth was trudging slowly, without enthusiasm, with his hands buried deep in his trousers' pockets, toward the down-town places where beds can be hired for coppers. He was clothed in an aged and tattered suit, and his derby was a marvel of dust-covered crown and torn rim. He was going forth to eat as the wanderer may eat, and sleep as the homeless sleep. By the time he had reached City Hall Park he was so completely plastered with yells of "bum" and "hobo," and with various unholy epithets that small boys had applied to him at intervals, that he was in a state of the most profound dejection. The sifting rain saturated the old velvet collar of his overcoat, and as the wet cloth pressed against his neck, he felt that there no longer could be pleasure in life. He looked about him searching for an outcast of highest degree that they too might share miseries, but the lights threw a quivering glare over rows and circles of deserted benches that glistened damply, showing patches of wet sod behind them. It seemed that their usual freights had fled on this night to better things. There were only squads of well-dressed Brooklyn people who swarmed towards the bridge.

The young man loitered about for a time and then went shuffling off down Park Row. In the sudden descent in style of the dress of the crowd he felt relief, and as if he were at last in his own country. He began to see tatters that matched his tatters. In Chatham Square there were aimless men strewn in front of saloons and lodging-houses, standing sadly, patiently, reminding one vaguely of the attitudes of chickens in a storm. He aligned himself with these men, and turned slowly to occupy himself with the flowing life of the great street.

Through the mists of the cold and storming night, the cable cars went in silent procession, great affairs shining with red and brass, moving with formidable power, calm and irresistible, dangerful and gloomy, breaking silence only by the loud fierce cry of the gong. Two rivers of people swarmed along the sidewalks, spattered with black mud, which made each shoe leave a scarlike impression. Overhead elevated trains with a shrill grinding of the wheels stopped at the station, which upon its leglike pillars seemed to resemble some monstrous kind of crab squatting over the street. The quick fat puffings of the engines could be heard. Down an alley there were somber curtains of purple and black, on which street lamps dully glittered like embroidered flowers.

A saloon stood with a voracious air on a corner. A sign leaning against the front of the door-post announced "Free hot soup to-night!" The swing doors, snapping to and fro like ravenous lips, made gratified smacks as the saloon gorged itself with plump men, eating with astounding and endless appetite, smiling in some indescribable manner as the men came from all directions like sacrifices to a heathenish superstition.

Caught by the delectable sign the young man allowed himself to be swallowed. A bartender placed a schooner of dark and portentous beer on the bar. Its monumental form up-reared until the froth a-top was above the crown of the young man's brown derby.

"Soup over there, gents," said the bartender affably. A little yellow man in rags and the youth grasped their schoon-ers and went with speed toward a lunch counter, where a man with oily but imposing whiskers ladled genially from a kettle until he had furnished his two mendicants with a soup that was steaming hot, and in which there were little float-ing suggestions of chicken. The young man, sipping his broth, felt the cordiality expressed by the warmth of the mixture, and he beamed at the man with oily but imposing whiskers, who was presiding like a priest behind an altar. "Have some more, gents?" he inquired of the two sorry figures before him. The little yellow man accepted with a swift gesture, but the youth shook his head and went out, following a man whose wondrous seediness promised that he would have a knowledge of cheap lodging-houses.

On the sidewalk he accosted the seedy man. "Say, do you know a cheap place to sleep?"

The other hesitated for a time, gazing sideways. Finally he nodded in the direction of the street, "I sleep up there," he said, "when I've got the price."

"How much?"

"Ten cents."

The young man shook his head dolefully. "That's too rich for me."

At that moment there approached the two a reeling man in strange garments. His head was a fuddle of bushy hair and whiskers, from which his eyes peered with a guilty slant. In a close scrutiny it was possible to distinguish the cruel lines of a mouth which looked as if its lips had just closed with satisfaction over some tender and piteous morsel. He appeared like an assassin steeped in crimes performed awkwardly.

But at this time his voice was tuned to the coaxing key of an affectionate puppy. He looked at the men with wheedling eyes, and began to sing a little melody for charity.

"Say, gents, can't yeh give a poor feller a couple of cents t' git a bed? I got five, and I gits anudder two I gits me a bed. Now, on th' square, gents, can't yeh jest gimme two cents t' git a bed? Now, yeh know how a respecter'ble gentlem'n feels when he's down on his luck, an' I——"

The seedy man, staring with imperturbable countenance at a train which clattered overhead, interrupted in an expressionless voice—"Ah, go t' h——!"

But the youth spoke to the prayerful assassin in tones of astonishment and inquiry. "Say, you must be crazy! Why don't yeh strike somebody that looks as if they had money?"

The assassin, tottering about on his uncertain legs, and at intervals brushing imaginary obstacles from before his nose, entered into a long explanation of the psychology of the situation. It was so profound that it was unintelligible.

When he had exhausted the subject, the young man said to him:

"Let's see th' five cents."

The assassin wore an expression of drunken woe at this sentence, filled with suspicion of him. With a deeply pained air he began to fumble in his clothing, his red hands trembling. Presently he announced in a voice of bitter grief, as if he had been betrayed—"There's on'y four."

"Four," said the young man thoughtfully. "Well, look here, I'm a stranger here, an' if ye'll steer me to your cheap joint I'll find the other three."

The assassin's countenance became instantly radiant with joy. His whiskers quivered with the wealth of his alleged emotions. He seized the young man's hand in a transport of delight and friendliness.

"B' Gawd," he cried, "if ye'll do that, b' Gawd, I'd say yeh was a damned good fellow, I would, an' I'd remember yeh all m' life, I would, b' Gawd, an' if I ever got a chance I'd return the compliment"—he spoke with drunken dignity —"b' Gawd, I'd treat yeh white, I would, an' I'd allus remember yeh."

The young man drew back, looking at the assassin coldly. "Oh, that's all right," he said. "You show me th' joint— that's all you've got t' do."

The assassin, gesticulating gratitude, led the young man along a dark street. Finally he stopped before a little dusty door. He raised his hand impressively. "Look-a-here," he said, and there was a thrill of deep and ancient wisdom upon his face, "I've brought yeh here, an' that's my part, ain't it? If th' place don't suit yeh, yeh needn't git mad at me, need yeh? There won't be no bad feelin', will there?"

"No," said the young man.

The assassin waved his arm tragically, and led the march up the steep stairway. On the way the young man furnished the assassin with three pennies. At the top a man with benevolent spectacles looked at them through a hole in a board. He collected their money, wrote some names on a register, and speedily was leading the two men along a gloom-shrouded corridor.

Shortly after the beginning of this journey the young man felt his liver turn white, for from the dark and secret places of the building there suddenly came to his nostrils strange and unspeakable odors, that assailed him like malignant diseases with wings. They seemed to be from human bodies closely packed in dens; the exhalations from a hundred pairs of reeking lips; the fumes from a thousand bygone debauches; the expression of a thousand present miseries.

A man, naked save for a little snuff-colored undershirt, was parading sleepily along the corridor. He rubbed his eyes, and, giving vent to a prodigious yawn, demanded to be told the time.

"Half-past one."

The man yawned again. He opened a door, and for a moment his form was outlined against a black, opaque interior. To this door came the three men, and as it was again opened the unholy odors rushed out like fiends, so that the young man was obliged to struggle as against an overpowering wind.

It was some time before the youth's eyes were good in the intense gloom within, but the man with benevolent spectacles led him skilfully, pausing but a moment to deposit the limp assassin upon a cot. He took the youth to a cot that lay tranquilly by the window, and showing him a tall locker for clothes that stood near the head with the ominous air of a tombstone, left him.

The youth sat on his cot and peered about him. There was a gas-jet in a distant part of the room, that burned a small flickering orange-hued flame. It caused vast masses of tumbled shadows in all parts of the place, save where, immediately about it, there was a little grey haze. As the young man's eyes became used to the darkness, he could see upon the cots that thickly littered the floor the forms of men sprawled out, lying in deathlike silence, or heaving and snoring with tremendous effort, like stabbed fish.

The youth locked his derby and his shoes in the mummy case near him, and then lay down with an old and familiar coat around his shoulders. A blanket he handed gingerly, drawing it over part of the coat. The cot was covered with leather, and as cold as melting snow. The youth was obliged to shiver for some time on this affair, which was like a slab. Presently, however, his chill gave him peace, and during this period of leisure from it he turned his head to stare at his friend the assassin, whom he could dimly discern where he lay sprawled on a cot in the abandon of a man filled with drink. He was snoring with incredible vigor. His wet hair and beard dimly glistened, and his inflamed nose shone with subdued lustre like a red light in a fog.

Within reach of the youth's hand was one who lay with yellow breast and shoulders bare to the cold drafts. One arm hung over the side of the cot, and the fingers lay full length upon the wet cement floor of the room. Beneath the inky brows could be seen the eyes of the man exposed by the partly opened lids. To the youth it seemed that he and this corpse-like being were exchanging a prolonged stare, and that the other threatened with his eyes. He drew back,

watching his neighbor from the shadows of his blanket edge.
The man did not move once through the night, but lay in
this stillness as of death like a body stretched out expectant
of the surgeon's knife.

And all through the room could be seen the tawny hues
of naked flesh, limbs thrust into the darkness, projecting
beyond the cots; upreared knees, arms hanging long and
thin over the cot edges. For the most part they were statu-
esque, carven, dead. With the curious lockers standing all
about like tombstones, there was a strange effect of a grave-
yard where bodies were merely flung.

Yet occasionally could be seen limbs wildly tossing in
fantastic nightmare gestures, accompanied by guttural cries,
grunts, oaths. And there was one fellow off in a gloomy
corner, who in his dreams was oppressed by some frightful
calamity, for of a sudden he began to utter long wails that
went almost like yells from a hound, echoing wailfully and
weird through this chill place of tombstones where men lay
like the dead.

The sound in its high piercing beginnings, that dwindled
to final melancholy moans, expressed a red and grim tragedy
of the unfathomable possibilities of the man's dreams. But
to the youth these were not merely the shrieks of a vision-
pierced man: they were an utterance of the meaning of the
room and its occupants. It was to him the protest of the
wretch who feels the touch of the imperturbable granite
wheels, and who then cries with an impersonal eloquence,
with a strength not from him, giving voice to the wail of a
whole section, a class, a people. This, weaving into the young
man's brain, and mingling with his views of the vast and

sombre shadows that, like mighty black fingers, curled around the naked bodies, made the young man so that he did not sleep, but lay carving the biographies for these men from his meagre experience. At times the fellow in the corner howled in a writhing agony of his imaginations.

Finally a long lance-point of grey light shot through the dusty panes of the window. Without, the young man could see roofs drearily white in the dawning. The point of light yellowed and grew brighter, until the golden rays of the morning sun came in bravely and strong. They touched with radiant color the form of a small fat man, who snored in stuttering fashion. His round and shiny bald head glowed suddenly with the valor of a decoration. He sat up, blinked at the sun, swore fretfully, and pulled his blanket over the ornamental splendors of his head.

The youth contentedly watched this rout of the shadows before the bright spears of the sun, and presently he slumbered. When he awoke he heard the voice of the assassin raised in valiant curses. Putting up his head, he perceived his comrade seated on the side of the cot engaged in scratching his neck with long finger-nails that rasped like files.

"Hully Jee, dis is a new breed. They've got can-openers on their feet." He continued in a violent tirade.

The young man hastily unlocked his closet and took out his shoes and hat. As he sat on the side of the cot lacing his shoes, he glanced about and saw that daylight had made the room comparatively commonplace and uninteresting. The men, whose faces seemed stolid, serene or absent, were engaged in dressing, while a great crackle of bantering conversation arose.

A few were parading in unconcerned nakedness. Here and there were men of brawn, whose skins shone clear and ruddy. They took splendid poses, standing massively like chiefs. When they had dressed in their ungainly garments there was an extraordinary change. They then showed bumps and deficiencies of all kinds.

There were others who exhibited many deformities. Shoulders were slanting, humped, pulled this way and pulled that way. And notable among these latter men was the little fat man who had refused to allow his head to be glorified. His pudgy form, builded like a pear, bustled to and fro, while he swore in fishwife fashion. It appeared that some article of his apparel had vanished.

The young man attired speedily, and went to his friend the assassin. At first the latter looked dazed at the sight of the youth. This face seemed to be appealing to him through the cloud wastes of his memory. He scratched his neck and reflected. At last he grinned, a broad smile gradually spreading until his countenance was a round illumination. "Hello, Willie," he cried cheerily.

"Hello," said the young man. "Are yeh ready t' fly?"

"Sure." The assassin tied his shoe carefully with some twine and came ambling.

When he reached the street the young man experienced no sudden relief from unholy atmospheres. He had forgotten all about them, and had been breathing naturally, and with no sensation of discomfort or distress.

He was thinking of these things as he walked along the street, when he was suddenly startled by feeling the assassin's hand, trembling with excitement, clutching his arm, and when the assassin spoke, his voice went into quavers from a supreme agitation.

"I'll be hully, bloomin' blowed if there wasn't a feller with a nightshirt on up there in that joint."

The youth was bewildered for a moment, but presently he turned to smile indulgently at the assassin's humor.

"Oh, you're a d——d liar," he merely said.

Whereupon the assassin began to gesture extravagantly, and take oath by strange gods. He frantically placed himself at the mercy of remarkable fates if his tale were not true.

"Yes, he did! I cross m' heart thousan' times!" he protested, and at the moment his eyes were large with amazement, his mouth wrinkled in unnatural glee.

"Yessir! A nightshirt! A hully white nightshirt!"

"You lie!"

"No, sir! I hope ter die b'fore I kin git anudder ball if there wasn't a jay wid a hully, bloomin' white nightshirt!"

His face was filled with the infinite wonder of it. "A hully white nightshirt," he continually repeated.

The young man saw the dark entrance to a basement restaurant. There was a sign which read "No mystery about our hash"! and there were other age-stained and world-battered legends which told him that the place was within his means. He stopped before it and spoke to the assassin. "I guess I'll git somethin' t' eat."

At this the assassin, for some reason, appeared to be quite embarrassed. He gazed at the seductive front of the eating place for a moment. Then he started slowly up the street. "Well, good-bye, Willie," he said bravely.

For an instant the youth studied the departing figure.

Then he called out, "Hol' on a minnet." As they came together he spoke in a certain fierce way, as if he feared that the other would think him to be charitable. "Look-a-here, if yeh wanta git some breakfas' I'll lend yeh three cents t' do it with. But say, look-a-here, you've gota git out an' hustle. I ain't goin' t' support yeh, or I'll go broke b'fore night. I ain't no millionaire."

"I take me oath, Willie," said the assassin earnestly, "th' on'y thing I really needs is a ball. Me t'roat feels like a fryin'-pan. But as I can't get a ball, why, th' next bes' thing is breakfast, an' if yeh do that for me, b' Gawd, I say yeh was th' whitest lad I ever see."

They spent a few moments in dexterous exchanges of phrases, in which they each protested that the other was, as the assassin had originally said, "a respecter'ble gentlem'n." And they concluded with mutual assurances that they were the souls of intelligence and virtue. Then they went into the restaurant.

There was a long counter, dimly lighted from hidden sources. Two or three men in soiled white aprons rushed here and there.

The youth bought a bowl of coffee for two cents and a roll for one cent. The assassin purchased the same. The bowls were webbed with brown seams, and the tin spoons wore an air of having emerged from the first pyramid. Upon them were black mosslike encrustations of age, and they were bent and scarred from the attacks of long-forgotten teeth. But over their repast the wanderers waxed warm and mellow. The assassin grew affable as the hot mixture went soothingly down his parched throat, and the young man felt courage flow in his veins.

Memories began to throng in on the asssasin, and he brought forth long tales, intricate, incoherent, delivered with a chattering swiftness as from an old woman. "——great job out'n Orange. Boss keep yeh hustlin' though all time. I was there three days, and then I went an' ask 'im t' lend me a dollar. 'G-g-go ter the. devil,' he ses, an' I lose me job."

"South no good. Damn niggers work for twenty-five an' thirty cents a day. Run white man out. Good grub, though. Easy livin'."

"Yas; useter work little in Toledo, raftin' logs. Make two or three dollars er day in the spring. Lived high. Cold as ice, though, in the winter."

"I was raised in northern N'York. O-a-ah, yeh jest oughto live there. No beer ner whisky, though, way off in the woods. But all th' good hot grub yeh can eat. B'Gawd, I hung around there long as I could till th' ol' man fired me. 'Git t' hell outa here, yeh wuthless skunk, git t' hell outa here, an' go die,' he ses. 'You're a hell of a father,' I ses, 'you are,' an' I quit 'im."

As they were passing from the dim eating place, they encountered an old man who was trying to steal forth with a tiny package of food, but a tall man with an indomitable moustache stood dragon fashion, barring the way of escape. They heard the old man raise a plaintive protest. "Ah, you always want to know what I take out, and you never see that I usually bring a package in here from my place of business."

As the wanderers trudged slowly along Park Row, the assassin began to expand and grow blithe. "B'Gawd, we've been livin' like kings," he said, smacking appreciative lips.

"Look out, or we'll have t' pay fer it t'night," said the youth with gloomy warning.

But the assassin refused to turn his gaze toward the future. He went with a limping step, into which he injected a suggestion of lamblike gambols. His mouth was wreathed in a red grin.

In the City Hall Park the two wanderers sat down in the little circle of benches sanctified by traditions of their class. They huddled in their old garments, slumbrously conscious of the march of the hours which for them had no meaning.

The people of the street hurrying hither and thither made a blend of black figures changing yet frieze-like. They walked in their good clothes as upon important missions, giving no gaze to the two wanderers seated upon the benches. They expressed to the young man his infinite distance from all that he valued. Social position, comfort, the pleasures of living, were unconquerable kingdoms. He felt a sudden awe.

And in the background a multitude of buildings, of pitiless hues and sternly high, were to him emblematic of a nation forcing its regal head into the clouds, throwing no downward glances; in the sublimity of its aspirations ignoring the wretches who may flounder at its feet. The roar of the city in his ear was to him the confusion of strange tongues, babbling heedlessly; it was the clink of coin, the voice of the city's hopes which were to him no hopes.

He confessed himself an outcast, and his eyes from under the lowered rim of his hat began to glance guiltily, wearing the criminal expression that comes with certain convictions.

THE DUEL THAT WAS NOT FOUGHT

THE DUEL THAT WAS NOT FOUGHT

PATSY TULLIGAN was not as wise as seven owls, but his courage could throw a shadow as long as the steeple of a cathedral. There were men on Cherry Street who had whipped him five times, but they all knew that Patsy would be as ready for the sixth time as if nothing had happened.

Once he and two friends had been away up on Eighth Avenue, far out of their country, and upon their return journey that evening they stopped frequently in saloons until they were as independent of their surroundings as eagles, and cared much less about thirty days on Blackwell's.

On Lower Sixth Avenue they paused in a saloon where there was a good deal of lamp-glare and polished wood to be seen from the outside, and within, the mellow light shone on much furbished brass and more polished wood. It was a better saloon than they were in the habit of seeing, but they did not mind it. They sat down at one of the little tables that were in a row parallel to the bar and ordered beer. They blinked stolidly at the decorations, the bartender, and the other customers. When anything transpired they discussed it with dazzling frankness, and what they said of it was as free as air to the other people in the place.

At midnight there were few people in the saloon. Patsy and his friends still sat drinking. Two well-dressed men were at another table, smoking cigars slowly and swinging back in their chairs. They occupied themselves with themselves in the usual manner, never betraying by a wink of an eyelid that they knew that other folk existed. At another table directly behind Patsy and his companions was a slim little Cuban, with miraculously small feet and hands, and with a youthful touch of down upon his lip. As he lifted his cigarette from time to time his little finger was bended in dainty fashion, and there was a green flash when a huge emerald ring caught the light. The bartender came often with his little brass tray. Occasionally Patsy and his two friends quarrelled.

Once this little Cuban happened to make some slight noise and Patsy turned his head to observe him. Then Patsy made a careless and rather loud comment to his two friends. He used a word which is no more than passing the time of day down in Cherry Street, but to the Cuban it was a dagger-point. There was a harsh scraping sound as a chair was pushed swiftly back.

The little Cuban was upon his feet. His eyes were shining with a rage that flashed there like sparks as he glared at Patsy. His olive face had turned a shade of grey from his anger. Withal his chest was thrust out in portentous dignity, and his hand, still grasping his wine-glass, was cool and steady, the little finger still bended, the great emerald gleaming upon it. The others, motionless, stared at him.

"Sir," he began ceremoniously. He spoke gravely and in a slow way, his tone coming in a marvel of self-possessed cadences from between those lips which quivered with wrath. You have insult me. You are a dog, a hound, a cur. I spit upon you. I must have some of your blood."

Patsy looked at him over his shoulder.

"What's th' matter wi' che?" he demanded. He did not quite understand the words of this little man who glared at him steadily, but he knew that it was something about fighting. He snarled with the readiness of his class and heaved his shoulders contemptuously. "Ah, what's eatin' yeh? Take a walk! You hain't got nothin' t' do with me, have yeh? Well, den, go sit on yerself."

And his companions leaned back valorously in their chairs, and scrutinized this slim young fellow who was addressing Patsy.

"What's de little Dago chewin' about?"

"He wants t' scrap!"

"What!"

The Cuban listened with apparent composure. It was only when they laughed that his body cringed as if he was receiving lashes. Presently he put down his glass and walked over to their table. He proceeded always with the most impressive deliberation.

"Sir," he began again. "You have insult me. I must have s-s-satisfac-shone. I must have your body upon the point of my sword. In my country you would already be dead. I must have s-s-satisfac-shone."

Patsy had looked at the Cuban with a trifle of bewilderment. But at last his face began to grow dark with belligerency, his mouth curved in that wide sneer with which he would confront an angel of darkness. He arose suddenly in his seat and came towards the little Cuban. He was going to be impressive too.

"Say, young feller, if yeh go shootin' off yer face at me, I'll wipe d' joint wid yeh. What'cher gaffin' about, hey? Are yeh givin' me er jolly? Say, if yeh pick me up fer a cinch, I'll fool yeh. Dat's what! Don't take me fer no dead easy mug." And as he glowered at the little Cuban, he ended his oration with one eloquent word, "Nit!"

The bartender nervously polished his bar with a towel, and kept his eyes fastened upon the men. Occasionally he became transfixed with interest, leaning forward with one hand upon the edge of the bar and the other holding the towel grabbed in a lump, as if he had been turned into bronze when in the very act of polishing.

The Cuban did not move when Patsy came toward him and delivered his oration. At its conclusion he turned his livid face toward where, above him, Patsy was swaggering and heaving his shoulders in a consummate display of bravery and readiness. The Cuban, in his clear, tense tones, spoke one word. It was the bitter insult. It seemed fairly to spin from his lips and crackle in the air like breaking glass.

Every man save the little Cuban made an electric movement. Patsy roared a black oath and thrust himself forward until he towered almost directly above the other man. His fists were doubled into knots of bone and hard flesh. The Cuban had raised a steady finger.

"If you touch me wis your hand, I will keel you."

The two well-dressed men had come swiftly, uttering protesting cries. They suddenly intervened in this second of time in which Patsy had sprung forward and the Cuban had uttered his threat. The four men were now a tossing, arguing, violent group, one well-dressed man lecturing the Cuban, and the other holding off Patsy, who was now wild with rage, loudly repeating the Cuban's threat, and maneuvering and struggling to get at him for revenge's sake.

The bartender, feverishly scouring away with his towel, and at times pacing to and fro with nervous and excited tread, shouted out—

"Say, for heaven's sake, don't fight in here.   If yeh wanta fight, go out in the street and fight all yeh please.   But don't fight in here."

Patsy knew one only thing, and this he kept repeating:

"Well, he wants t' scrap!   I didn't begin dis!   He wants t' scrap."

The well-dressed man confronting him continually replied—

"Oh, well, now, look here, he's only a lad.   He don't know what he's doing.   He's crazy mad.   You wouldn't slug a kid like that."

Patsy and his aroused companions, who cursed and growled, were persistent with their argument.   "Well, he wants t' scrap!"   The whole affair was as plain as daylight when one saw this great fact.   The interference and intolerable discussion brought the three of them forward, battleful and fierce.

"What's eatin' you, anyhow?" they demanded.   "Dis ain't your business, is it?   What business you got shootin' off your face?"

The other peacemaker was trying to restrain the little Cuban, who had grown shrill and violent.

"If he touch me wis his hand I will keel him.   We must

fight like gentlemen or else I keel him when he touch me wis his hand."

The man who was fending off Patsy comprehended these sentences that were screamed behind his back, and he explained to Patsy.

"But he wants to fight you with swords. With swords, you know."

The Cuban, dodging around the peacemakers, yelled in Patsy's face—

"Ah, if I could get you before me wis my sword! Ah! Ah! A-a-ah!" Patsy made a furious blow with a swift fist, but the peacemakers bucked against his body suddenly like football players.

Patsy was greatly puzzled. He continued doggedly to try to get near enough to the Cuban to punch him. To these attempts the Cuban replied savagely—

"If you touch me wis your hand, I will cut your heart in two piece."

At last Patsy said—"Well, if he's so dead stuck on fightin' wid swords, I'll fight 'im. Soitenly! I'll fight 'im." All this palaver had evidently tired him, and he now puffed out his lips with the air of a man who is willing to submit to any conditions if he can only bring on the row soon enough. He swaggered, "I'll fight 'im wid swords. Let 'im bring on his swords, an' I'll fight 'im 'til he's ready t' quit."

The two well-dressed men grinned. "Why, look here," they said to Patsy, "he'd punch you full of holes. Why he's a fencer. You can't fight him with swords. He'd kill you in 'bout a minute."

"Well, I'll giv' 'im a go at it, anyhow," said Patsy, stout-hearted and resolute. "I'll giv' 'im a go at it, anyhow, an' I'll stay wid 'im as long as I kin."

As for the Cuban, his lithe body was quivering in an ecstasy of the muscles. His face radiant with a savage joy, he fastened his glance upon Patsy, his eyes gleaming with a gloating, murderous light. A most unspeakable, animal-like rage was in his expression.

"Ah! ah! He will fight me! Ah!" He bended unconsciously in the posture of a fencer. He had all the quick, springy movements of a skilful swordsman. "Ah, the b-r-r-rute! The b-r-r-rute! I will stick him like a pig!"

The two peacemakers, still grinning broadly, were having a great time with Patsy.

"Why, you infernal idiot, this man would slice you all up. You better jump off the bridge if you want to commit suicide. You wouldn't stand a ghost of a chance to live ten seconds."

Patsy was as unshaken as granite. "Well, if he wants t' fight wid swords, he'll get it. I'll giv' 'im a go at it, anyhow."

One man said—"Well, have you got a sword? Do you know what a sword is? Have you got a sword?"

"No, I ain't got none," said Patsy honestly, "but I kin git one." Then he added valiantly—"An' quick, too."

The two men laughed. "Why, can't you understand it would be sure death to fight a sword duel with this fellow?"

"Dat's all right! See? I know me own business. If he wants t' fight one of dees d—n duels, I'm in it, understan'?"

"Have you ever fought one, you fool?"

"No, I ain't. But I will fight one, dough! I ain't no muff. If he wants t' fight a duel, by Gawd, I'm wid 'im!

D'yeh understan' dat!" Patsy cocked his hat and swaggered. He was getting very serious.

The little Cuban burst out—"Ah, come on, sirs: come on! We can take cab. Ah, you big cow, I will stick you, I will stick you. Ah, you will look very beautiful, very beautiful. Ah, come on, sirs. We will stop at hotel—my hotel. I there have weapons."

"Yeh will, will yeh? Yeh bloomin' little black Dago!" cried Patsy in hoarse and maddened reply to the personal part of the Cuban's speech. He stepped forward. "Git yer d—n swords," he commanded. "Git yer swords. Git 'em quick! I'll fight wi' che! I'll fight wid anyt'ing, too! See? I'll fight yeh wid a knife an' fork if yeh say so! I'll fight yer standin' up er sittin' down!" Patsy delivered this intense oration with sweeping, intensely emphatic gestures, his hands stretched out eloquently, his jaw thrust forward, his eyes glaring.

"Ah!" cried the little Cuban joyously. "Ah, you are in very pretty temper. Ah, how I will cut your heart in two piece, my dear, d-e-a-r friend." His eyes, too, shone like carbuncles, with a swift, changing glitter, always fastened upon Patsy's face.

The two peacemakers were perspiring and in despair. One of them blurted out—

"Well, I'll be blamed if this ain't the most ridiculous thing I ever saw."

The other said—"For ten dollars I'd be tempted to let these two infernal blockheads have their duel."

Patsy was strutting to and fro, and conferring grandly with his friends.

"He took me for a muff. He t'ought he was goin' t' bluff me out, talkin' 'bout swords. He'll get fooled." He addressed the Cuban—"You're a fine little dirty picter of a scrapper, ain't che? I'll chew yez up, dat's what I will!"

There began then some rapid action. The patience of well-dressed men is not an eternal thing. It began to look as if it would at last be a fight with six corners to it. The faces of the men were shining red with anger. They jostled each other defiantly, and almost every one blazed out at three or four of the others. The bartender had given up protesting. He swore for a time and banged his glasses. Then he jumped the bar and ran out of the saloon, cursing sullenly.

When he came back with a policeman, Patsy and the Cuban were preparing to depart together. Patsy was delivering his last oration—

"I'll fight yer wid swords! Sure I will! Come ahead, Dago! I'll fight yeh anywheres wid anyt'ing! We'll have a large, juicy scrap, an' don't yeh forgit dat! I'm right wid yez. I ain't no muff! I scrap with a man jest as soon as he ses scrap, an' if yeh wanta scrap, I'm yer kitten. Understan' dat?"

The policeman said sharply—"Come, now; what's all this?" He had a distinctly business air.

The little Cuban stepped forward calmly. "It is none of your business."

The policeman flushed to his ears. "What?"

One well-dressed man touched the other on the sleeve. "Here's the time to skip," he whispered. They halted a block away from the saloon and watched the policeman pull the Cuban through the door. There was a minute of scuffle on the sidewalk, and into this deserted street at midnight fifty people appeared at once as if from the sky to watch it.

At last the three Cherry Hill men came from the saloon, and swaggered with all their old valor toward the peace-makers.

"Ah," said Patsy to them, "he was so hot talkin' about this duel business, but I would a-given 'im a great scrap, an' don't yeh forgit it."

For Patsy was not as wise as seven owls, but his courage could throw a shadow as long as the steeple of a cathedral.

A DESERTION

A DESERTION

THE yellow gaslight that came with an effect of difficulty through the dust-stained windows on either side of the door gave strange hues to the faces and forms of the three women who stood gabbling in the hallway of the tenement. They made rapid gestures, and in the background their enormous shadows mingled in terrific conflict.

"Aye, she ain't so good as he thinks she is, I'll bet. He can watch over 'er an' take care of 'er all he pleases, but when she wants t' fool 'im, she'll fool 'im. An' how does he know she ain't foolin' im' now?"

"Oh, he thinks he's keepin' 'er from goin' t' th' bad, he does. Oh, yes. He ses she's too purty t' let run round alone. Too purty! Huh! My Sadie——"

"Well, he keeps a clost watch on 'er, you bet. On'y las' week, she met my boy Tim on th' stairs, an' Tim hadn't said two words to 'er b'fore th' ol' man begin to holler. "Dorter, dorter, come here, come here!'"

At this moment a young girl entered from the street, and it was evident from the injured expression suddenly assumed by the three gossipers that she had been the object of their discussion. She passed them with a slight nod, and they swung about into a row to stare after her.

On her way up the long flights the girl unfastened her veil. One could then clearly see the beauty of her eyes,

but there was in them a certain furtiveness that came near
to marring the effects. It was a peculiar fixture of gaze,
brought from the street, as of one who there saw a succession of passing dangers with menaces aligned at every corner.

On the top floor, she pushed open a door and then paused
on the threshold, confronting an interior that appeared black
and flat like a curtain. Perhaps some girlish idea of hob-
goblins assailed her then, for she called in a little breathless
voice, "Daddie!"

There was no reply. The fire in the cooking-stove in the
room crackled at spasmodic intervals. One lid was mis-
placed, and the girl could now see that this fact created a
little flushed crescent upon the ceiling. Also, a series of
tiny windows in the stove caused patches of red upon the
floor. Otherwise, the room was heavily draped with shadows.

The girl called again, "Daddie!"

Yet there was no reply.

"Oh, Daddie!"

Presently she laughed as one familiar with the humors of
an old man. "Oh, I guess yer cussin' mad about yer supper, Dad," she said, and she almost entered the room, but
suddenly faltered, overcome by a feminine instinct to fly
from this black interior, peopled with imagined dangers.

Again she called, "Daddie!" Her voice had an accent of
appeal. It was as if she knew she was foolish but yet felt
obliged to insist upon being reassured. "Oh, Daddie!"

Of a sudden a cry of relief, a feminine announcement that
the stars still hung, burst from her. For, according to some
mystic process, the smoldering coals of the fire went aflame
with sudden, fierce brilliance, splashing parts of the walls, the

floor, the crude furniture, with a hue of blood-red. And in the light of this dramatic outburst of light, the girl saw her father seated at a table with his back turned toward her.

She entered the room, then, with an aggrieved air, her logic evidently concluding that somebody was to blame for her nervous fright. "Oh, yer on'y sulkin' 'bout yer supper. I thought mebbe ye'd gone somewheres."

Her father made no reply. She went over to a shelf in the corner, and, taking a little lamp, she lit it and put it where it would give her light as she took off her hat and jacket in front of the tiny mirror. Presently she began to bustle among the cooking utensils that were crowded into the sink, and as she worked she rattled talk at her father, apparently disdaining his mood.

"I'd 'a' come home earlier t'night, Dad, on'y that fly foreman, he kep' me in th' shop 'til half-past six. What a fool! He came t' me, yeh know, an' he ses, 'Nell, I wanta give yeh some brotherly advice.' Oh, I know him an' his brotherly advice. 'I wanta give yeh some brotherly advice. Yer too purty, Nell,' he ses, ''t' be workin' in this shop an' paradin' through the streets alone, without somebody t' give yeh good brotherly advice, an' I wanta warn yeh, Nell. I'm a bad man, but I ain't as bad as some, an' I wanta warn yeh.' 'Oh, g'long 'bout yer business,' I ses. I know 'im. He's like all of 'em, on'y he's a little slyer. I know 'im. 'You g'long 'bout yer business,' I ses. Well, he ses after a while that he guessed some evenin' he'd come up an' see me. 'Oh, yeh will,' I ses, 'yeh will? Well, you jest let my ol' man ketch yeh comin' foolin' 'round our place. Yeh'll wish yeh went t' some other girl t' give brotherly advice.' 'What th' 'ell do I care fer yer father?' he ses. 'What's he t' me?' 'If he throws yeh downstairs, yeh'll care for 'im,' I ses. 'Well,' he ses, 'I'll come when 'e ain't in, b' Gawd, I'll come when 'e ain't in.' 'Oh, he's allus in when it means takin' care 'o me,' I ses. 'Don't yeh fergit it, either. When it comes t' takin' care o' his dorter, he's right on deck every single possible time.' "

After a time, she turned and addressed cheery words to the old man. "Hurry up th' fire, Daddie! We'll have supper pretty soon."

But still her father was silent, and his form in its sullen posture was motionless.

At this, the girl seemed to see the need of the inauguration of a feminine war against a man out of temper. She approached him breathing soft, coaxing syllables.

"Daddie! Oh, Daddie! O—o—oh, Daddie!"

It was apparent from a subtle quality of valor in her tones that this manner of onslaught upon his moods had usually been successful, but to-night it had no quick effect. The words, coming from her lips, were like the refrain of an old ballad, but the man remained stolid.

"Daddie! My Daddie! Oh, Daddie, are yeh mad at me, really—truly mad at me!"

She touched him lightly upon the arm. Should he have turned then he would have seen the fresh, laughing face, with dew-sparkling eyes, close to his own.

"Oh, Daddie! My Daddie! Pretty Daddie!"

She stole her arm about his neck, and then slowly bended her face toward his. It was the action of a queen who knows that she reigns notwithstanding irritations, trials, tempests.

But suddenly, from this position, she leaped backward with the mad energy of a frightened colt. Her face was in this instant turned to a grey, featureless thing of horror. A yell, wild and hoarse as a brute-cry, burst from her. "Daddie!" She flung herself to a place near the door, where she remained, crouching, her eyes staring at the motionless figure, spattered by the quivering flashes from the fire. Her arms extended, and her frantic fingers at once besought and repelled. There was in them an expression of eagerness to caress and an expression of the most intense loathing. And the girl's hair that had been a splendor, was in these moments changed to a disordered mass that hung and swayed in witchlike fashion.

Again, a terrible cry burst from her. It was more than the shriek of agony—it was directed, personal, addressed to him in the chair, the first word of a tragic conversation with the dead.

It seemed that when she had put her arm about its neck, she had jostled the corpse in such a way that now she and it were face to face. The attitude expressed an intention of arising from the table. The eyes, fixed upon hers, were filled with an unspeakable hatred.

*   *   *   *   *   *   *

The cries of the girl aroused thunders in the tenement. There was a loud slamming of doors, and presently there was a roar of feet upon the boards of the stairway. Voices rang out sharply.

"What is it?"

"What's th' matter?"

"He's killin' her!"

"Slug 'im with anythin' yeh kin lay hold of, Jack!"

But over all this came the shrill, shrewish tones of a woman. "Ah, th' damned ol' fool, he's drivin' 'er inteh th' street—that's what he's doin'. He's drivin' 'er inteh th' street."

A DARK-BROWN DOG

A DARK-BROWN DOG

A CHILD was standing on a street-corner. He leaned with one shoulder against a high board fence and swayed the other to and fro, the while kicking carelessly at the gravel.

Sunshine beat upon the cobbles, and a lazy summer wind raised yellow dust which trailed in clouds down the avenue. Clattering trucks moved with indistinctness through it. The child stood dreamily gazing.

After a time, a little dark-brown dog came trotting with an intent air down the sidewalk. A short rope was dragging from his neck. Occasionally he trod upon the end of it and stumbled.

He stopped opposite the child, and the two regarded each other. The dog hesitated for a moment, but presently he made some little advances with his tail. The child put out his hand and called him. In an apologetic manner the dog came close, and the two had an interchange of friendly pattings and waggles. The dog became more enthusiastic with each moment of the interview, until with his gleeful caperings he threatened to overturn the child. Whereupon the child lifted his hand and struck the dog a blow upon the head.

This thing seemed to overpower and astonish the little dark-brown dog, and wounded him to the heart. He sank down in despair at the child's feet. When the blow was repeated, together with an admonition in childish sentences, he turned over upon his back, and held his paws in a peculiar manner. At the same time with his ears and his eyes he offered a small prayer to the child.

He looked so comical on his back, and holding his paws peculiarly, that the child was greatly amused and gave him little taps repeatedly, to keep him so. But the little dark-brown dog took this chastisement in the most serious way, and no doubt considered that he had committed some grave crime, for he wriggled contritely and showed his repentance in every way that was in his power. He pleaded with the child and petitioned him, and offered more prayers.

At last the child grew weary of this amusement and turned toward home. The dog was praying at the time. He lay on his back and turned his eyes upon the retreating form.

Presently he struggled to his feet and started after the child. The latter wandered in a perfunctory way toward his home, stopping at times to investigate various matters. During one of these pauses he discovered the little dark-brown dog who was following him with the air of a footpad.

The child beat his pursuer with a small stick he had found. The dog lay down and prayed until the child had finished, and resumed his journey. Then he scrambled erect and took up the pursuit again.

On the way to his home the child turned many times and beat the dog, proclaiming with childish gestures that he held him in contempt as an unimportant dog, with no value save for a moment. For being this quality of animal the dog apologized and eloquently expressed regret, but he continued stealthily to follow the child. His manner grew so very guilty that he slunk like an assassin.

When the child reached his doorstep, the dog was industriously ambling a few yards in the rear. He became so agitated with shame when he again confronted the child that he forgot the dragging rope. He tripped upon it and fell forward.

The child sat down on the step and the two had another interview. During it the dog greatly exerted himself to please the child. He performed a few gambols with such abandon that the child suddenly saw him to be a valuable thing. He made a swift, avaricious charge and seized the rope.

He dragged his captive into a hall and up many long stairways in a dark tenement. The dog made willing efforts, but he could not hobble very skilfully up the stairs because he was very small and soft, and at last the pace of the engrossed child grew so energetic that the dog became panic-stricken. In his mind he was being dragged toward a grim unknown. His eyes grew wild with the terror of it. He began to wiggle his head frantically and to brace his legs.

The child redoubled his exertions. They had a battle on the stairs. The child was victorious because he was completely absorbed in his purpose, and because the dog was very small. He dragged his acquirement to the door of his home, and finally with triumph across the threshold.

No one was in. The child sat down on the floor and made overtures to the dog. These the dog instantly accepted. He beamed with affection upon his new friend. In a short time they were firm and abiding comrades.

When the child's family appeared, they made a great row. The dog was examined and commented upon and called names. Scorn was leveled at him from all eyes, so that he became much embarrassed and drooped like a scorched plant. But the child went sturdily to the center of the floor, and, at the top of his voice, championed the dog. It happened that he was roaring protestations, with his arms clasped about the dog's neck, when the father of the family came in from work.

The parent demanded to know what the blazes they were making the kid howl for. It was explained in many words that the infernal kid wanted to introduce a disreputable dog into the family.

A family council was held. On this depended the dog's fate, but he in no way heeded, being busily engaged in chewing the end of the child's dress.

The affair was quickly ended. The father of the family, it appears, was in a particularly savage temper that evening, and when he perceived that it would amaze and anger everybody if such a dog were allowed to remain, he decided that it should be so. The child, crying softly, took his friend off to a retired part of the room to hobnob with him, while the father quelled a fierce rebellion of his wife. So it came to pass that the dog was a member of the household.

He and the child were associated together at all times save when the child slept. The child became a guardian and a friend. If the large folk kicked the dog and threw things at him, the child made loud and violent objections. Once when the child had run, protesting loudly, with tears raining down his face and his arms outstretched, to protect his

friend, he had been struck in the head with a very large
saucepan from the hand of his father, enraged at some seem-
ing lack of courtesy in the dog. Ever after, the family were
careful how they threw things at the dog. Moreover, the
latter grew very skilful in avoiding missiles and feet. In a
small room containing a stove, a table, a bureau and some
chairs, he would display strategic ability of a high order,
dodging, feinting and scuttling about among the furniture.
He could force three or four people armed with brooms,
sticks and handfuls of coal, to use all their ingenuity to get
in a blow. And even when they did, it was seldom that they
could do him a serious injury or leave any imprint.

But when the child was present these scenes did not occur. It came to be recognized that if the dog was molested,
the child would burst into sobs, and as the child, when
started, was very riotous and practically unquenchable, the
dog had therein a safeguard.

However, the child could not always be near. At night,
when he was asleep, his dark-brown friend would raise from
some black corner a wild, wailful cry, a song of infinite lone-
liness and despair, that would go shuddering and sobbing
among the buildings of the block and cause people to swear.
At these times the singer would often be chased all over the
kitchen and hit with a great variety of articles.

Sometimes, too, the child himself used to beat the dog,
although it is not known that he ever had what truly could
be called a just cause. The dog always accepted these
thrashings with an air of admitted guilt. He was too much
of a dog to try to look to be a martyr or to plot revenge. He
received the blows with deep humility, and furthermore he

forgave his friend the moment the child had finished, and was ready to caress the child's hand with his little red tongue.

When misfortune came upon the child, and his troubles overwhelmed him, he would often crawl under the table and lay his small distressed head on the dog's back. The dog was ever sympathetic. It is not to be supposed that at such times he took occasion to refer to the unjust beatings his friend, when provoked, had administered to him.

He did not achieve any notable degree of intimacy with the other members of the family. He had no confidence in them, and the fear that he would express at their casual approach often exasperated them exceedingly. They used to gain a certain satisfaction in underfeeding him, but finally his friend the child grew to watch the matter with some care, and when he forgot it, the dog was often successful in secret for himself.

So the dog prospered. He developed a large bark, which came wondrously from such a small rug of a dog. He ceased to howl persistently at night. Sometimes, indeed, in his sleep, he would utter little yells, as from pain, but that occurred, no doubt, when in his dreams he encountered huge flaming dogs who threatened him direfully.

His devotion to the child grew until it was a sublime thing. He wagged at his approach; he sank down in despair at his departure. He could detect the sound of the child's step among all the noises of the neighborhood. It was like a calling voice to him.

The scene of their companionship was a kingdom governed by this terrible potentate, the child; but neither criticism nor rebellion ever lived for an instant in the heart of the one subject. Down in the mystic, hidden fields of his little dog-soul bloomed flowers of love and fidelity and perfect faith.

The child was in the habit of going on many expeditions to observe strange things in the vicinity. On these occasions his friend usually jogged aimfully along behind. Perhaps, though, he went ahead. This necessitated his turning around every quarter-minute to make sure the child was coming. He was filled with a large idea of the importance of these journeys. He would carry himself with such an air! He was proud to be the retainer of so great a monarch.

One day, however, the father of the family got quite exceptionally drunk. He came home and held carnival with the cooking utensils, the furniture and his wife. He was in the midst of this recreation when the child, followed by the darkbrown dog, entered the room. They were returning from their voyages.

The child's practised eye instantly noted his father's state. He dived under the table, where experience had taught him was a rather safe place. The dog, lacking skill in such matters, was, of course, unaware of the true condition of affairs. He looked with interested eyes at his friend's sudden dive. He interpreted it to mean: Joyous gambol. He started to patter across the floor to join him. He was the picture of a little dark-brown dog en route to a friend.

The head of the family saw him at this moment. He gave a huge howl of joy, and knocked the dog down with a heavy coffee-pot. The dog, yelling in supreme astonishment and fear, writhed to his feet and ran for cover. The man kicked out with a ponderous foot. It caused the dog to swerve as if caught in a tide.   A second blow of the coffee-pot laid him upon the floor.

Here the child, uttering loud cries, came valiantly forth like a knight.   The father of the family paid no attention to these calls of the child, but advanced with glee upon the dog.   Upon being knocked down twice in swift succession, the latter apparently gave up all hope of escape.   He rolled over on his back and held his paws in a peculiar manner.   At the same time with his eyes and his ears he offered up a small prayer.

But the father was in a mood for having fun, and it occurred to him that it would be a fine thing to throw the dog out of the window.   So he reached down and, grabbing the animal by a leg, lifted him, squirming, up.   He swung him two or three times hilariously about his head, and then flung him with great accuracy through the window.

The soaring dog created a surprise in the block.   A woman watering plants in an opposite window gave an involuntary shout and dropped a flower-pot.   A man in another window leaned perilously out to watch the flight of the dog.   A woman who had been hanging out clothes in a yard began to caper wildly.   Her mouth was filled with clothes-pins, but her arms gave vent to a sort of exclamation.   In appearance she was like a gagged prisoner.   Children ran whooping.

The dark-brown body crashed in a heap on the roof of a shed five stories below.   From thence it rolled to the pavement of an alleyway.

The child in the room far above burst into a long, dirge-like cry, and toddled hastily out of the room.   It took him a long time to reach the alley, because his size compelled him to go downstairs backward, one step at a time, and holding with both hands to the step above.

When they came for him later, they found him seated by the body of his dark-brown friend.

THE PACE OF YOUTH

THE PACE OF YOUTH

I

STIMSON stood in a corner and glowered. He was a fierce man and had indomitable whiskers, albeit he was very small.

"That young tarrier," he whispered to himself. "He wants to quit makin' eyes at Lizzie. This is too much of a good thing. First thing you know, he'll get fired."

His brow creased in a frown, he strode over to the huge open doors and looked at a sign. "Stimson's Mammoth Merry-Go-Round," it read, and the glory of it was great. Stimson stood and contemplated the sign. It was an enormous affair; the letters were as large as men. The glow of it, the grandeur of it was very apparent to Stimson. At the end of his contemplation, he shook his head thoughtfully, determinedly. "No, no," he muttered. "This is too much of a good thing. First thing you know, he'll get fired."

A soft booming sound of surf, mingled with the cries of bathers, came from the beach. There was a vista of sand and sky and sea that drew to a mystic point far away in the northward. In the mighty angle, a girl in a red dress was crawling slowly like some kind of a spider on the fabric of nature. A few flags hung lazily above where the bath-houses were marshalled in compact squares. Upon the edge of the sea stood a ship with its shadowy sails painted dimly upon the sky, and high overhead in the still, sun-shot air a great hawk swung and drifted slowly.

Within the Merry-Go-Round there was a whirling circle of ornamental lions, giraffes, camels, ponies, goats, glittering with varnish and metal that caught swift reflections from windows high above them. With stiff wooden legs, they swept on in a never-ending race, while a great orchestrion clamored in wild speed. The summer sunlight sprinkled its gold upon the garnet canopies carried by the tireless racers and upon all the devices of decoration that made Stimson's machine magnificent and famous. A host of laughing children bestrode the animals, bending forward like charging cavalrymen, and shaking reins and whooping in glee. At intervals they leaned out perilously to clutch at iron rings that were tendered to them by a long wooden arm. At the intense moment before the swift grab for the rings one could see their little nervous bodies quiver with eagerness; the laughter rang shrill and excited. Down in the long rows of benches, crowds of people sat watching the game, while occasionally a father might arise and go near to shout encouragement, cautionary commands, or applause at his flying offspring. Frequently mothers called out: "Be careful, Georgie!" The orchestrion bellowed and thundered on its platform, filling the ears with its long monotonous song. Over in a corner, a man in a white apron and behind a counter roared above the tumult: "Pop corn! Pop corn!"

A young man stood upon a small, raised platform, erected in a manner of a pulpit, and just without the line of the circling figures. It was his duty to manipulate the wooden arm and affix the rings. When all were gone into the hands of the triumphant children, he held forth a basket, into which they returned all save the coveted brass one, which meant another ride free and made the holder very illustrious. The young man stood all day upon his narrow platform, affixing rings or holding forth the basket. He was a sort of general squire in these lists of childhood. He was very busy.

And yet Stimson, the astute, had noticed that the young man frequently found time to twist about on his platform and smile at a girl who shyly sold tickets behind a silvered netting. This, indeed, was the great reason of Stimson's glowering. The young man upon the raised platform had no manner of license to smile at the girl behind the silvered netting. It was a most gigantic insolence. Stimson was amazed at it. "By Jiminy," he said to himself again, "that fellow is smiling at my daughter." Even in this tone of great wrath it could be discerned that Stimson was filled with wonder that any youth should dare smile at the daughter in the presence of the august father.

Often the dark-eyed girl peered between the shining wires, and, upon being detected by the young man, she usually turned her head quickly to prove to him that she was not interested. At other times, however, her eyes seemed filled with a tender fear lest he should fall from that exceedingly dangerous platform. As for the young man, it was plain that these glances filled him with valor, and he stood carelessly upon his perch, as if he deemed it of no consequence that he might fall from it. In all the complexities of his daily life and duties he found opportunity to gaze ardently at the vision behind the netting.

This silent courtship was conducted over the heads of the crowd who thronged about the bright machine. The swift eloquent glances of the young man went noiselessly and unseen with their message. There had finally become established between the two in this manner a subtle understanding and companionship. They communicated accurately all that they felt. The boy told his love, his reverence, his hope in the changes of the future. The girl told him that she loved him, and she did not love him, that she did not know if she loved him. Sometimes a little sign saying "cashier" in gold letters, and hanging upon the silvered netting, got directly in range and interfered with the tender message.

The love affair had not continued without anger, unhappiness, despair. The girl had once smiled brightly upon a youth who came to buy some tickets for his little sister, and the young man upon the platform, observing this smile, had been filled with gloomy rage. He stood like a dark statue of vengeance upon his pedestal and thrust out the basket to the children with a gesture that was full of scorn for their hollow happiness, for their insecure and temporary joy. For five hours he did not once look at the girl when she was looking at him. He was going to crush her with his indifference; he was going to demonstrate that he had never been serious. However, when he narrowly observed her in secret he discovered that she seemed more blythe than was usual with her. When he found that his apparent indifference had not crushed her he suffered greatly. She did not love him, he concluded. If she had loved him she would have been crushed. For two days he lived a miserable existence upon his high perch. He consoled himself by thinking of how unhappy he was, and by swift, furtive glances at the loved face. At any rate he was in her presence, and he could get a good view from his perch when there was no interference by the little sign: "Cashier."

But suddenly, swiftly, these clouds vanished, and under the imperial blue sky of the restored confidence they dwelt in peace, a peace that was satisfaction, a peace that, like a babe, put its trust in the treachery of the future. This confidence endured until the next day, when she, for an unknown cause, suddenly refused to look at him. Mechanically he continued his task, his brain dazed, a tortured victim of doubt, fear, suspicion. With his eyes he supplicated her to telegraph an explanation. She replied with a stony glance that froze his blood. There was a great difference in their respective reasons for becoming angry. His were always foolish, but apparent, plain as the moon. Hers were subtle, feminine, as incomprehensible as the stars, as mysterious as the shadows at night.

They fell and soared and soared and fell in this manner until they knew that to live without each other would be a wandering in deserts. They had grown so intent upon the uncertainties, the variations, the guessings of their affair that the world had become but a huge immaterial background. In time of peace their smiles were soft and prayerful, caresses confided to the air. In time of war, their youthful hearts, capable of profound agony, were wrung by the intricate emotions of doubt. They were the victims of the dread angel of affectionate speculation that forces the brain endlessly on roads that lead nowhere.

At night, the problem of whether she loved him confronted the young man like a spectre, looming as high as a hill and telling him not to delude himself. Upon the following day, this battle of the night displayed itself in the renewed fervor of his glances and in their increased number. Whenever he thought he could detect that she too was suffering, he felt a thrill of joy.

But there came a time when the young man looked back upon these contortions with contempt. He believed then that he had imagined his pain. This came about when the redoubtable Stimson marched forward to participate.

"This has got to stop," Stimson had said to himself, as he stood and watched them. They had grown careless of the light world that clattered about them; they were become so engrossed in their personal drama that the language of their eyes was almost as obvious as gestures. And Stimson, through his keenness, his wonderful, infallible penetration, suddenly came into possession of these obvious facts. "Well, of all the nerves," he said, regarding with a new interest the young man upon the perch.

He was a resolute man. He never hesitated to grapple with a crisis. He decided to overturn everything at once, for, although small, he was very fierce and impetuous. He resolved to crush this dreaming.

He strode over to the silvered netting. "Say, you want to quit your everlasting grinning at that idiot," he said, grimly.

The girl cast down her eyes and made a little heap of quarters into a stack. She was unable to withstand the terrible scrutiny of her small and fierce father.

Stimson turned from his daughter and went to a spot beneath the platform. He fixed his eyes upon the young man and said—

"I've been speakin' to Lizzie. You better attend strictly to your own business or there'll be a new man here next week." It was as if he had blazed away with a shotgun. The young man reeled upon his perch. At last he in a measure regained his composure and managed to stammer: "A—all right, sir." He knew that denials would be futile with the terrible Stimson. He agitatedly began to rattle the rings in the basket, and pretend that he was obliged to count them or inspect them in some way. He, too, was unable to face the great Stimson.

For a moment, Stimson stood in fine satisfaction and gloated over the effect of his threat.

"I've fixed them," he said complacently, and went out to smoke a cigar and revel in himself. Through his mind went the proud reflection that people who came in contact with his granite will usually ended in quick and abject submission.

II

ONE evening, a week after Stimson had indulged in the proud reflection that people who came in contact with his granite will usually ended in quick and abject submission, a young feminine friend of the girl behind the silvered netting came to her there and asked her to walk on the beach after "Stimson's Mammoth Merry-Go-Round" was closed for the night. The girl assented with a nod.

The young man upon the perch holding the rings saw this nod and judged its meaning. Into his mind came an idea of defeating the watchfulness of the redoubtable Stimson.

When the Merry-Go-Round was closed and the two girls started for the beach, he wandered off aimlessly in another direction, but he kept them in view, and as soon as he was assured that he had escaped the vigilance of Stimson, he followed them.

The electric lights on the beach made a broad band of tremoring light, extending parallel to the sea, and upon the wide walk there slowly paraded a great crowd, intermingling, interwining, sometimes colliding. In the darkness stretched the vast purple expanse of the ocean, and the deep indigo sky above was peopled with yellow stars. Occasionally out upon the water a whirling mass of froth suddenly flashed into view, like a great ghostly robe appearing, and then vanished, leaving the sea in its darkness, whence came those bass tones of the water's unknown emotion. A wind, cool, reminiscent of the wave wastes, made the women hold their wraps about their throats, and caused the men to grip the rims of their straw hats. It carried the noise of the band in the pavilion in gusts. Sometimes people unable to hear the music glanced up at the pavilion and were reassured upon beholding the distant leader still gesticulating and bobbing, and the other members of the band with their lips glued to their instruments. High in the sky soared an unassuming moon, faintly silver.

For a time the young man was afraid to approach the two girls; he followed them at a distance and called himself a coward. At last, however, he saw them stop on the outer edge of the crowd and stand silently listening to the voices of the sea. When he came to where they stood, he was trembling in his agitation. They had not seen him.

"Lizzie," he began. "I——"

The girl wheeled instantly and put her hand to her throat. "Oh, Frank, how you frightened me," she said—inevitably.

"Well, you know, I—I——" he stuttered.

But the other girl was one of those beings who are born to attend at tragedies. She had for love a reverence, an admiration that was greater the more that she contemplated the fact that she knew nothing of it. This couple, with their emotions, awed her and made her humbly wish that she might be destined to be of some service to them. She was very homely.

When the young man faltered before them, she, in her sympathy, actually over-estimated the crisis, and felt that he might fall dying at their feet. Shyly, but with courage, she marched to the rescue.

"Won't you come and walk on the beach with us?" she said.

The young man gave her a glance of deep gratitude which was not without the patronage which a man in his condition naturally feels for one who pities it. The three walked on.

Finally, the being who was born to attend at this tragedy said that she wished to sit down and gaze at the sea, alone.

They politely urged her to walk on with them, but she was obstinate. She wished to gaze at the sea, alone. The young man swore to himself that he would be her friend until he died.

And so the two young lovers went on without her. They turned once to look at her.

"Jennie's awful nice," said the girl.

"You bet she is," replied the young man, ardently.

They were silent for a little time.

At last the girl said—

"You were angry at me yesterday."

"No, I wasn't."

"Yes, you were, too. You wouldn't look at me once all day."

"No, I wasn't angry. I was only putting on."

Though she had, of course, known it, this confession seemed to make her very indignant. She flashed a resentful glance at him.

"Oh, you were, indeed?" she said with a great air.

For a few minutes she was so haughty with him that he loved her to madness. And directly this poem, which stuck at his lips, came forth lamely in fragments.

When they walked back toward the other girl and saw the patience of her attitude, their hearts swelled in a patronizing and secondary tenderness for her.

They were very happy. If they had been miserable they would have charged this fairy scene of the night with a criminal heartlessness; but as they were joyous, they vaguely wondered how the purple sea, the yellow stars, the changing crowds under the electric lights could be so phlegmatic and stolid.

They walked home by the lakeside way, and out upon the water those gay paper lanterns, flashing, fleeting, and careering, sang to them, sang a chorus of red and violet, and green and gold; a song of mystic bands of the future.

One day, when business paused during a dull sultry afternoon, Stimson went up town. Upon his return, he found that the popcorn man, from his stand over in a corner, was keeping an eye upon the cashier's cage, and that nobody at all was attending to the wooden arm and the iron rings. He strode forward like a sergeant of grenadiers.

"Where in thunder is Lizzie?" he demanded, a cloud of rage in his eyes.

The popcorn man, although associated long with Stimson, had never got over being dazed.

"They've—they've—gone round to th'—th'—house," he said with difficulty, as if he had just been stunned.

"Whose house?" snapped Stimson.

"Your—your house, I s'pose," said the popcorn man.

Stimson marched round to his home. Kingly denunciations surged, already formulated, to the tip of his tongue, and he bided the moment when his anger could fall upon the heads of that pair of children. He found his wife convulsive and in tears.

"Where's Lizzie?"

And then she burst forth—"Oh—John—John—they've run away, I know they have. They drove by here not three minutes ago. They must have done it on purpose to bid me good-bye, for Lizzie waved her hand sadlike; and then, before I could get out to ask where they were going or what, Frank whipped up the horse."

Stimson gave vent to a dreadful roar.

"Get my revolver—get a hack—get my revolver, do you hear—what the devil——" His voice became incoherent.

He had always ordered his wife about as if she were a battalion of infantry, and despite her misery, the training of years forced her to spring mechanically to obey; but suddenly she turned to him with a shrill appeal.

"Oh, John—not—the—revolver."

"Confound it, let go of me!" he roared again, and shook her from him.

He ran hatless upon the street. There were a multitude of hacks at the summer resort, but it was ages to him before he could find one. Then he charged it like a bull.

"Uptown!" he yelled, as he tumbled into the rear seat.

The hackman thought of severed arteries. His galloping horse distanced a large number of citizens who had been running to find what caused such contortions by the little hatless man.

It chanced as the bouncing hack went along near the lake, Stimson gazed across the calm grey expanse and recognized a color in a bonnet and a pose of a head. A buggy was traveling along a highway that led to Sorington. Stimson bellowed—"There—there—there they are—in that buggy."

The hackman became inspired with the full knowledge of the situation. He struck a delirious blow with the whip. His mouth expanded in a grin of excitement and joy. It came to pass that this old vehicle, with its drowsy horse and its dusty-eyed and tranquil driver, seemed suddenly to awaken, to become animated and fleet. The horse ceased to ruminate on his state, his air of reflection vanished. He became intent upon his aged legs and spread them in quaint and ridiculous devices for speed. The driver, his eyes shining, sat critically in his seat. He watched each motion of this rattling machine down before him. He resembled an engineer. He used the whip with judgment and deliberation as the engineer would have used coal or oil. The horse clacked swiftly upon the macadam, the wheels hummed, the body of the vehicle wheezed and groaned.

Stimson, in the rear seat, was erect in that impassive attitude that comes sometimes to the furious man when he is obliged to leave the battle to others. Frequently, however, the tempest in his breast came to his face and he howled—

"Go it—go it—you're gaining; pound 'im! Thump the life out of 'im; hit 'im hard, you fool!" His hand grasped the rod that supported the carriage top, and it was clenched so that the nails were faintly blue.

Ahead, that other carriage had been flying with speed, as from realization of the menace in the rear. It bowled away rapidly, drawn by the eager spirit of a young and modern horse. Stimson could see the buggy-top bobbing, bobbing. That little pane, like an eye, was a derision to him. Once he leaned forward and bawled angry sentences. He began to feel impotent; his whole expedition was a tottering of an old man upon a trail of birds. A sense of age made him choke again with wrath. That other vehicle, that was youth, with youth's pace; it was swift-flying with the hope of dreams. He began to comprehend those two children ahead of him, and he knew a sudden and strange awe, because he understood the power of their young blood, the power to fly strongly into the future and feel and hope again, even at that time when his bones must be laid in the earth. The dust rose easily from the hot road and stifled the nostrils of Stimson.

The highway vanished far away in a point with a suggestion of intolerable length. The other vehicle was becoming so small that Stimson could no longer see the derisive eye.

At last the hackman drew rein to his horse and turned to look at Stimson.

"No use, I guess," he said.

Stimson made a gesture of acquiescence, rage, despair. As the hackman turned his dripping horse about, Stimson sank back with the astonishment and grief of a man who has been defied by the universe. He had been in a great perspiration, and now his bald head felt cool and uncomfortable. He put up his hand with a sudden recollection that he had forgotten his hat.

At last he made a gesture. It meant that at any rate he was not responsible.

A TENT IN AGONY

A TENT IN AGONY

A SULLIVAN COUNTY TALE

FOUR men once came to a wet place in the roadless forest to fish. They pitched their tent fair upon the brow of a pine-clothed ridge of riven rocks whence a bowlder could be made to crash through the brush and whirl past the trees to the lake below. On fragrant hemlock boughs they slept the sleep of unsuccessful fishermen, for upon the lake alternately the sun made them lazy and the rain made them wet. Finally they ate the last bit of bacon and smoked and burned the last fearful and wonderful hoecake.

Immediately a little man volunteered to stay and hold the camp while the remaining three should go the Sullivan county miles to a farmhouse for supplies. They gazed at him dismally. "There's only one of you—the devil make a twin," they said in parting malediction, and disappeared down the hill in the known direction of a distant cabin. When it came night and the hemlocks began to sob they had not returned. The little man sat close to his companion, the campfire, and encouraged it with logs. He puffed fiercely at a heavy built brier, and regarded a thousand shadows which were about to assault him. Suddenly he heard the approach of the unknown, crackling the twigs and rustling the dead leaves. The little man arose slowly to his feet, his clothes refused to fit his back, his pipe dropped from his mouth, his knees

177

smote each other. "Hah!" he bellowed hoarsely in menace.
A growl replied and a bear paced into the light of the fire.
The little man supported himself upon a sapling and regarded
his visitor.

The bear was evidently a veteran and a fighter, for the
black of his coat had become tawny with age. There was
confidence in his gait and arrogance in his small, twinkling
eye. He rolled back his lips and disclosed his white teeth.
The fire magnified the red of his mouth. The little man had
never before confronted the terrible and he could not wrest
it from his breast. "Hah!" he roared. The bear interpreted
this as the challenge of a gladiator. He approached warily.
As he came near, the boots of fear were suddenly upon the
little man's feet. He cried out and then darted around the
campfire. "Ho!" said the bear to himself, "this thing won't
fight—it runs. Well, suppose I catch it." So upon his features there fixed the animal look of going—somewhere. He
started intensely around the campfire. The little man
shrieked and ran furiously. Twice around they went.

The hand of heaven sometimes falls heavily upon the
righteous. The bear gained.

In desperation the little man flew into the tent. The
bear stopped and sniffed at the entrance. He scented the
scent of many men. Finally he ventured in.

The little man crouched in a distant corner. The bear advanced, creeping, his blood burning, his hair erect, his jowls
dripping. The little man yelled and rustled clumsily under
the flap at the end of the tent. The bear snarled awfully
and made a jump and a grab at his disappearing game. The
little man, now without the tent, felt a tremendous paw

grab his coat tails. He squirmed and wriggled out of his coat like a schoolboy in the hands of an avenger. The bear howled triumphantly and jerked the coat into the tent and took two bites, a punch and a hug before he discovered his man was not in it. Then he grew not very angry, for a bear on a spree is not a black-haired pirate. He is merely a hoodlum. He lay down on his back, took the coat on his four paws and began to play uproariously with it. The most appalling, blood-curdling whoops and yells came to where the little man was crying in a treetop and froze his blood. He moaned a little speech meant for a prayer and clung convulsively to the bending branches. He gazed with tearful wistfulness at where his comrade, the campfire, was giving dying flickers and crackles. Finally, there was a roar from the tent which eclipsed all roars; a snarl which it seemed would shake the stolid silence of the mountain and cause it to shrug its granite shoulders. The little man quaked and shrivelled to a grip and a pair of eyes. In the glow of the embers he saw the white tent quiver and fall with a crash. The bear's merry play had disturbed the center pole and brought a chaos of canvas upon his head.

Now the little man became the witness of a mighty scene. The tent began to flounder. It took flopping strides in the direction of the lake. Marvellous sounds came from within —rips and tears, and great groans and pants. The little man went into giggling hysterics.

The entangled monster failed to extricate himself before he had walloped the tent frenziedly to the edge of the mountain. So it came to pass that three men, clambering up the hill with bundles and baskets, saw their tent approaching.

It seemed to them like a white-robed phantom pursued by hornets. Its moans riffled the hemlock twigs.

The three men dropped their bundles and scurried to one side, their eyes gleaming with fear. The canvas avalanche swept past them. They leaned, faint and dumb, against trees and listened, their blood stagnant. Below them it struck the base of a great pine tree, where it writhed and struggled. The three watched its convolutions a moment and then started terrifically for the top of the hill. As they disappeared, the bear cut loose with a mighty effort. He cast one dishevelled and agonized look at the white thing, and then started wildly for the inner recesses of the forest.

The three fear-stricken individuals ran to the rebuilt fire. The little man reposed by it calmly smoking. They sprang at him and overwhelmed him with interrogations. He contemplated darkness and took a long, pompous puff. "There's only one of me—and the devil made a twin," he said.

FOUR MEN IN A CAVE

FOUR MEN IN A CAVE

LIKEWISE FOUR QUEENS, AND A SULLIVAN COUNTY
HERMIT

THE moon rested for a moment on the top of a tall pine on a hill.

The little man was standing in front of the campfire making orations to his companions.

"We can tell a great tale when we get back to the city if we investigate this thing," said he, in conclusion.

They were won.

The little man was determined to explore a cave, because its black mouth had gaped at him. The four men took a lighted pine-knot and clambered over boulders down a hill. In a thicket on the mountainside lay a little tilted hole. At its side they halted.

"Well?" said the little man.

They fought for last place and the little man was overwhelmed. He tried to struggle from under by crying that if the fat, pudgy man came after, he would be corked. But he finally administered a cursing over his shoulder and crawled into the hole. His companions gingerly followed.

A passage, the floor of damp clay and pebbles, the walls slimy, green-mossed, and dripping, sloped downward. In the

183

cave atmosphere the torches became studies in red blaze and black smoke.

"Ho!" cried the little man, stifled and bedraggled, "let's go back." His companions were not brave. They were last. The next one to the little man pushed him on, so the little man said sulphurous words and cautiously continued his crawl.

Things that hung seemed to be on the wet, uneven ceiling, ready to drop upon the men's bare necks. Under their hands the clammy floor seemed alive and writhing. When the little man endeavored to stand erect the ceiling forced him down. Knobs and points came out and punched him. His clothes were wet and mud-covered, and his eyes, nearly blinded by smoke, tried to pierce the darkness always before his torch.

"Oh, I say, you fellows, let's go back," cried he. At that moment he caught the gleam of trembling light in the blurred shadows before him.

"Ho!" he said, "here's another way out."

The passage turned abruptly. The little man put one hand around the corner, but it touched nothing. He investigated and discovered that the little corridor took a sudden dip down a hill. At the bottom shone a yellow light.

The little man wriggled painfully about, and descended feet in advance. The others followed his plan. All picked their way with anxious care. The traitorous rocks rolled from beneath the little man's feet and roared thunderously below him, lesser stone loosened by the men above him, hit him on the back. He gained seemingly firm foothold, and, turning halfway about, swore redly at his companions for dolts and careless fools. The pudgy man sat, puffing and perspiring, high in the rear of the procession. The fumes and smoke from four pine-knots were in his blood. Cinders and sparks lay thick in his eyes and hair. The pause of the little man angered him.

"Go on, you fool!" he shouted. "Poor, painted man, you are afraid."

"Ho!" said the little man. "Come down here and go on yourself, imbecile!"

The pudgy man vibrated with passion. He leaned downward. "Idiot——"

He was interrupted by one of his feet which flew out and crashed into the man in front of and below. It is not well to quarrel upon a slippery incline, when the unknown is below. The fat man, having lost the support of one pillar-like foot, lurched forward. His body smote the next man, who hurtled into the next man. Then they all fell upon the cursing little man.

They slid in a body down over the slippery, slimy floor of the passage. The stone avenue must have wibble-wobbled with the rush of this ball of tangled men and strangled cries. The torches went out with the combined assault upon the little man. The adventurers whirled to the unknown in darkness. The little man felt that he was pitching to death, but even in his convolutions he bit and scratched at his companions, for he was satisfied that it was their fault. The swirling mass went some twenty feet, and lit upon a level, dry place in a strong, yellow light of candles. It dissolved and became eyes.

The four men lay in a heap upon the floor of a grey

chamber. A small fire smoldered in the corner, the smoke
disappearing in a crack. In another corner was a bed of
faded hemlock boughs and two blankets. Cooking utensils
and clothes lay about, with boxes and a barrel.

Of these things the four men took small cognisance. The
pudgy man did not curse the little man, nor did the little
man swear, in the abstract. Eight widened eyes were fixed
upon the center of the room of rocks.

A great, gray stone, cut squarely, like an altar, sat in the
middle of the floor. Over it burned three candles, in swaying tin cups hung from the ceiling. Before it, with what
seemed to be a small volume clasped in his yellow fingers
stood a man. He was an infinitely sallow person in the
brown-checked shirt of the ploughs and cows. The rest of
his apparel was boots. A long grey beard dangled from his
chin. He fixed glinting, fiery eyes upon the heap of men
and remained motionless. Fascinated, their tongues cleav-
ing, their blood cold, they arose to their feet. The gleaming
glance of the recluse swept slowly over the group until it
found the face of the little man. There it stayed and burned

The little man shrivelled and crumpled as the dried leaf
under the glass.

Finally, the recluse slowly, deeply spoke. It was a true
voice from a cave, cold, solemn, and damp.

"It's your ante," he said.

"What?" said the little man.

The hermit tilted his beard and laughed a laugh that was
either the chatter of a banshee in a storm or the rattle of
pebbles in a tin box. His visitors' flesh seemed ready to
drop from their bones.

They huddled together and cast fearful eyes over their shoulders. They whispered.

"A vampire!" said one.

"A ghoul!" said another.

"A Druid before the sacrifice," murmured another.

"The shade of an Aztec witch doctor," said the little man.

As they looked, the inscrutable face underwent a change. It became a livid background for his eyes, which blazed at the little man like impassioned carbuncles. His voice arose to a howl of ferocity. "It's your ante!" With a panther-like motion he drew a long, thin knife and advanced, stooping. Two cadaverous hounds came from nowhere, and, scowling and growling, made desperate feints at the little man's legs. His quaking companions pushed him forward.

Tremblingly he put his hand to his pocket.

"How much?" he said, with a shivering look at the knife that glittered.

The carbuncles faded.

"Three dollars," said the hermit, in sepulchral tones which rang against the walls and among the passages, awakening long-dead spirits with voices. The shaking little man took a roll of bills from a pocket and placed "three ones" upon the altar-like stone. The recluse looked at the little volume with reverence in his eyes. It was a pack of playing cards.

Under the three swinging candles, upon the altar-like stone, the grey beard and the agonized little man played at poker. The three other men crouched in a corner, and stared with eyes that gleamed with terror. Before them sat the cadaverous hounds licking their red lips. The candles burned low, and began to flicker. The fire in the corner expired.

Finally, the game came to a point where the little man laid down his hand and quavered: "I can't call you this time, sir. I'm dead broke."

"What?" shrieked the recluse. "Not call me! Villain! Dastard! Cur! I have four queens, miscreant." His voice grew so mighty that it could not fit his throat. He choked, wrestling with his lungs for a moment. Then the power of his body was concentrated in a word: "Go!"

He pointed a quivering, yellow finger at a wide crack in the rock. The little man threw himself at it with a howl. His erstwhile frozen companions felt their blood throb again. With great bounds they plunged after the little man. A minute of scrambling, falling, and pushing brought them to open air. They climbed the distance to their camp in furious springs.

The sky in the east was a lurid yellow. In the west the footprints of departing night lay on the pine trees. In front of their replenished camp fire sat John Willerkins, the guide.

"Hello!" he shouted at their approach. "Be you fellers ready to go deer huntin'?"

Without replying, they stopped and debated among themselves in whispers.

Finally, the pudgy man came forward.

"John," he inquired, "do you know anything peculiar about this cave below here?"

"Yes," said Willerkins at once; "Tom Gardner."

"What?" said the pudgy man.

"Tom Gardner."

"How's that?"

"Well, you see," said Willerkins slowly, as he took digni-

fied pulls at his pipe, "Tom Gardner was once a fambly man,
who lived in these here parts on a nice leetle farm.   He uster
go away to the city orften, and one time he got a-gamblin'
in one of them there dens.   He went ter the dickens right
quick then.   At last he kum home one time and tol' his
folks he had up and sold the farm and all he had in the
worl'.   His leetle wife she died then.   Tom he went crazy,
and soon after—"

The narrative was interrupted by the little man, who became possessed of devils.

"I wouldn't give a cuss if he had left me 'nough money
to get home on the doggoned, grey-haired red pirate," he
shrilled, in a seething sentence.   The pudgy man gazed at
the little man calmly and sneeringly.

"Oh, well," he said, "we can tell a great tale when we get
back to the city after having investigated this thing."

"Go to the devil," replied the little man.

THE MESMERIC MOUNTAIN

THE MESMERIC MOUNTAIN

A TALE OF SULLIVAN COUNTY

On the brow of a pine-plumed hillock there sat a little man with his back against a tree. A venerable pipe hung from his mouth, and smoke-wreaths curled slowly skyward. He was muttering to himself with his eyes fixed on an irregular black opening in the green wall of forest at the foot of the hill. Two vague wagon ruts led into the shadows. The little man took his pipe in his hands and addressed the listening pines.

"I wonder what the devil it leads to," said he.

A grey, fat rabbit came lazily from a thicket and sat in the opening. Softly stroking his stomach with his paw, he looked at the little man in a thoughtful manner. The little man threw a stone, and the rabbit blinked and ran through an opening. Green, shadowy portals seemed to close behind him.

The little man started. "He's gone down that roadway," he said, with ecstatic mystery to the pines. He sat a long time and contemplated the door to the forest. Finally, he arose, and awakening his limbs, started away. But he stopped and looked back.

"I can't imagine what it leads to," muttered he. He trudged over the brown mats of pine needles, to where, in a

fringe of laurel, a tent was pitched, and merry flames caroused about some logs. A pudgy man was fuming over a
collection of tin dishes. He came forward and waved a
plate furiously in the little man's face.

"I've washed the dishes for three days. What do you
think I am—"

He ended a red oration with a roar: "Damned if I do
it any more."

The little man gazed dim-eyed away. "I've been wonderin' what it leads to."

"What?"

"That road out yonder. I've been wonderin' what it
leads to. Maybe, some discovery or something," said the
little man.

The pudgy man laughed. "You're an idiot. It leads to
ol' Jim Boyd's over on the Lumberland Pike."

"Ho!" said the little man, "I don't believe that."

The pudgy man swore. "Fool, what does it lead to, then?"

"I don't know just what, but I'm sure it leads to something great or something. It looks like it."

While the pudgy man was cursing, two more men came
from obscurity with fish dangling from birch twigs. The
pudgy man made an obviously herculean struggle and a meal
was prepared. As he was drinking his cup of coffee, he suddenly spilled it and swore. The little man was wandering
off.

"He's gone to look at that hole," cried the pudgy man.

The little man went to the edge of the pine-plumed hillock,
and, sitting down, began to make smoke and regard the door
to the forest. There was stillness for an hour. Compact

clouds hung unstirred in the sky. The pines stood motionless, and pondering.

Suddenly the little man slapped his knees and bit his tongue. He stood up and determinedly filled his pipe, rolling his eye over the bowl to the doorway. Keeping his eyes fixed he slid dangerously to the foot of the hillock and walked down the wagon ruts. A moment later he passed from the noise of the sunshine to the gloom of the woods.

The green portals closed, shutting out live things. The little man trudged on alone.

Tall tangled grass grew in the roadway, and the trees bended obstructing branches. The little man followed on over pine-clothed ridges and down through water-soaked swales. His shoes were cut by rocks of the mountains, and he sank ankle-deep in mud and moss of swamps. A curve just ahead lured him miles.

Finally, as he wended the side of a ridge, the road disappeared from beneath his feet. He battled with hordes of ignorant bushes on his way to knolls and solitary trees which invited him. Once he came to a tall, bearded pine. He climbed it, and perceived in the distance a peak. He uttered an ejaculation and fell out.

He scrambled to his feet, and said: "That's Jones's Mountain, I guess. It's about six miles from our camp as the crow flies."

He changed his course away from the mountain, and attacked the bushes again. He climbed over great logs, golden-brown in decay, and was opposed by thickets of dark-green laurel. A brook slid through the ooze of a swamp, cedars and hemlocks hung their spray to the edges of pools.

The little man began to stagger in his walk. After a time he stopped and mopped his brow.

"My legs are about to shrivel up and drop off," he said. . . . "Still if I keep on in this direction, I am safe to strike the Lumberland Pike before sundown."

He dived at a clump of tag-alders, and emerging, confronted Jones's Mountain.

The wanderer sat down in a clear space and fixed his eyes on the summit. His mouth opened widely, and his body swayed at times. The little man and the peak stared in silence.

A lazy lake lay asleep near the foot of the mountain. In its bed of water-grass some frogs leered at the sky and crooned. The sun sank in red silence, and the shadows of the pines grew formidable. The expectant hush of evening, as if some thing were going to sing a hymn, fell upon the peak and the little man.

A leaping pickerel off on the water created a silver circle that was lost in black shadows. The little man shook himself and started to his feet, crying: "For the love of Mike, there's eyes in this mountain! I feel 'em! Eyes!"

He fell on his face.

When he looked again, he immediately sprang erect and ran.

"It's comin'!"

The moutain was approaching.

The little man scurried, sobbing through the thick growth. He felt his brain turning to water. He vanquished brambles with mighty bounds.

But after a time he came again to the foot of the mountain.

"God!" he howled, "it's been follerin' me." He grovelled. Casting his eyes upward made circles swirl in his blood. "I'm shackled I guess," he moaned. As he felt the heel of the mountain about to crush his head, he sprang again to his feet. He grasped a handful of small stones and hurled them.

"Damn you," he shrieked loudly. The pebbles rang against the face of the mountain.

The little man then made an attack. He climbed with hands and feet wildly. Brambles forced him back and stones slid from beneath his feet. The peak swayed and tottered, and was ever about to smite with a granite arm. The summit was a blaze of red wrath.

But the little man at last reached the top. Immediately he swaggered with valor to the edge of the cliff. His hands were scornfully in his pockets.

He gazed at the western horizon, edged sharply against a yellow sky. "Ho!" he said. "There's Boyd's house and the Lumberland Pike."

The mountain under his feet was motionless.   (

THE SNAKE

THE SNAKE

WHERE the path wended across the ridge, the bushes of huckleberry and sweet fern swarmed at it in two curling waves until it was a mere winding line traced through a tangle. There was no interference by clouds, and as the rays of the sun fell full upon the ridge, they called into voice innumerable insects which chanted the heat of the summer day in steady, throbbing, unending chorus.

A man and a dog came from the laurel thickets of the valley where the white brook brawled with the rocks. They followed the deep line of the path across the ridges. The dog—a large lemon and white setter—walked, tranquilly meditative, at his master's heels.

Suddenly from some unknown and yet near place in advance there came a dry, shrill whistling rattle that smote motion instantly from the limbs of the man and the dog. Like the fingers of a sudden death, this sound seemed to touch the man at the nape of the neck, at the top of the spine, and change him, as swift as thought, to a statue of listening horror, surprise, rage. The dog, too—the same icy hand was laid upon him, and he stood crouched and quivering, his jaw dropping, the froth of terror upon his lips, the light of hatred in his eyes.

Slowly the man moved his hands toward the bushes, but

his glance did not turn from the place made sinister by the warning rattle. His fingers, unguided, sought for a stick of weight and strength. Presently they closed about one that seemed adequate, and holding this weapon poised before him, the man moved slowly forward, glaring. The dog with his nervous nostrils fairly fluttering moved warily, one foot at a time, after his master.

But when the man came upon the snake, his body underwent a shock as if from a revelation, as if after all he had been ambushed. With a blanched face, he sprang forward and his breath came in strained gasps, his chest heaving as if he were in the performance of an extraordinary muscular trial. His arm with the stick made a spasmodic, defensive gesture.

The snake had apparently been crossing the path in some mystic travel when to his sense there came the knowledge of the coming of his foes. The dull vibration perhaps informed him, and he flung his body to face the danger. He had no knowledge of paths; he had no wit to tell him to slink noiselessly into the bushes. He knew that his implacable enemies were approaching; no doubt they were seeking him, hunting him. And so he cried his cry, an incredibly swift jangle of tiny bells, as burdened with pathos as the hammering upon quaint cymbals by the Chinese at war—for, indeed, it was usually his death-music.

"Beware! Beware! Beware!"

The man and the snake confronted each other. In the man's eyes were hatred and fear. In the snake's eyes were hatred and fear. These enemies maneuvered, each preparing to kill. It was to be a battle without mercy. Neither knew of mercy for such a situation. In the man was all the wild strength of the terror of his ancestors, of his race, of his kind. A deadly repulsion had been handed from man to man through long dim centuries. This was another detail of a war that had begun evidently when first there were men and snakes. Individuals who do not participate in this strife incur the investigations of scientists. Once there was a man and a snake who were friends, and at the end, the man lay dead with the marks of the snake's caress just over his East Indian heart. In the formation of devices, hideous and horrible, Nature reached her supreme point in the making of the snake, so that priests who really paint hell well fill it with snakes instead of fire. The curving forms, these scintillant coloring create at once, upon sight, more relentless animosities than do shake barbaric tribes. To be born a snake is to be thrust into a place a-swarm with formidable foes. To gain an appreciation of it, view hell as pictured by priests who are really skilful.

As for this snake in the pathway, there was a double curve some inches back of its head, which, merely by the potency of its lines, made the man feel with tenfold eloquence the touch of the death-fingers at the nape of his neck. The reptile's head was waving slowly from side to side and its hot eyes flashed like little murder-lights. Always in the air was the dry, shrill whistling of the rattles.

"Beware! Beware! Beware!"

The man made a preliminary feint with his stick. Instantly the snake's heavy head and neck were bended back on the double curve and instantly the snake's body shot forward in a low, strait, hard spring. The man jumped with a convulsive chatter and swung his stick. The blind, sweeping blow fell upon the snake's head and hurled him so that steel-colored plates were for a moment uppermost. But he rallied swiftly, agilely, and again the head and neck bended back to the double curve, and the steaming, wide-open mouth made its desperate effort to reach its enemy. This attack, it could be seen, was despairing, but it was nevertheless impetuous, gallant, ferocious, of the same quality as the charge of the lone chief when the walls of white faces close upon him in the mountains. The stick swung unerringly again, and the snake, mutilated, torn, whirled himself into the last coil.

And now the man went sheer raving mad from the emotions of his forefathers and from his own. He came to close quarters. He gripped the stick with his two hands and made it speed like a flail. The snake, tumbling in the anguish of final despair, fought, bit, flung itself upon this stick which was taking his life.

At the end, the man clutched his stick and stood watching in silence. The dog came slowly and with infinite caution stretched his nose forward, sniffing. The hair upon his neck and back moved and ruffled as if a sharp wind was blowing. the last muscular quivers of the snake were causing the rattles to still sound their treble cry, the shrill, ringing war chant and hymn of the grave of the thing that faces foes at once countless, implacable, and superior.

"Well, Rover," said the man, turning to the dog with a grin of victory, "we'll carry Mr. Snake home to show the girls."

His hands still trembled from the strain of the encounter,

but he pried with his stick under the body of the snake and hoisted the limp thing upon it. He resumed his march along the path, and the dog walked tranquilly meditative, at his master's heels.

LONDON IMPRESSIONS

LONDON IMPRESSIONS

CHAPTER I

LONDON at first consisted of a porter with the most charming manners in the world, and a cabman with a supreme intelligence, both observing my profound ignorance without contempt or humor of any kind observable in their manners. It was in a great resounding vault of a place where there were many people who had come home, and I was displeased because they knew the detail of the business, whereas I was confronting the inscrutable. This made them appear very stony-hearted to the sufferings of one of whose existence, to be sure, they were entirely unaware, and I remember taking great pleasure in disliking them heartily for it. I was in an agony of mind over my baggage, or my luggage, or my— perhaps it is well to shy around this terrible international question; but I remember that when I was a lad I was told that there was a whole nation that said luggage instead of baggage, and my boyish mind was filled at the time with incredulity and scorn. In the present case it was a thing that I understood to involve the most hideous confessions of imbecility on my part, because I had evidently to go out to some obscure point and espy it and claim it, and take trouble for it; and I would rather have had my pockets filled with bread and cheese, and had no baggage at all.

Mind you, this was not at all a homage that I was paying to London. I was paying homage to a new game. A man properly lazy does not like new experiences until they become old ones. Moreover, I have been taught that a man, any man, who has a thousand times more points of information on a certain thing than I have will bully me because of it, and pour his advantages upon my bowed head until I am drenched with his superiority. It was in my education to concede some license of the kind in this case, but the holy father of a porter and the saintly cabman occupied the middle distance imperturbably, and did not come down from their hills to clout me with knowledge. From this fact I experienced a criminal elation. I lost view of the idea that if I had been brow-beaten by porters and cabmen from one end of the United States to the other end I should warmly like it, because in numbers they are superior to me, and collectively they can have a great deal of fun out of a matter that would merely afford me the glee of the latent butcher.

This London, composed of a porter and a cabman, stood to me subtly as a benefactor. I had scanned the drama, and found that I did not believe that the mood of the men emanated unduly from the feature that there was probably more shillings to the square inch of me than there were shillings to the square inch of them. Nor yet was it any manner of palpable warm-heartedness or other natural virtue. But it was a perfect artificial virtue; it was drill, plain, simple drill. And now was I glad of their drilling, and vividly approved of it, because I saw that it was good for me. Whether it was good or bad for the porter and the cabman I could not know; but that point, mark you, came within the pale of my respectable rumination.

I am sure that it would have been more correct for me

to have alighted upon St. Paul's and described no emotion until I was overcome by the Thames Embankment and the Houses of Parliament. But as a matter of fact I did not see them for some days, and at this time they did not concern me at all. I was born in London at a railroad station, and my new vision encompassed a porter and a cabman. They deeply absorbed me in new phenomena, and I did not then care to see the Thames Embankment nor the Houses of Parliament. I considered the porter and the cabman to be more important.

CHAPTER II

THE cab finally rolled out of the gas-lit vault into a vast expanse of gloom. This changed to the shadowy lines of a street that was like a passage in a monstrous cave. The lamps winking here and there resembled the little gleams at the caps of the miners. They were not very competent illuminations at best, merely being little pale flares of gas that at their most heroic periods could only display one fact concerning this tunnel—the fact of general direction. But at any rate I should have liked to have observed the dejection of a search-light if it had been called upon to attempt to bore through this atmosphere. In it each man sat in his own little cylinder of vision, so to speak. It was not so small as a sentry-box nor so large as a circus tent, but the walls were opaque, and what was passing beyond the dimensions of his cylinder no man knew.

It was evident that the paving was very greasy, but all the cabs that passed through my cylinder were going at a round trot, while the wheels, shod in rubber, whirred merely like bicycles. The hoofs of the animals themselves did not make that wild clatter which I knew so well. New York, in fact, roars always like ten thousand devils. We have ingenuous and simple ways of making a din in New York that cause the stranger to conclude that each citizen is obliged by statute to provide himself with a pair of cymbals and a drum. If anything by chance can be turned into a noise it is promptly turned. We are engaged in the development of a human creature with very large, sturdy, and doubly-fortified ears.

It was not too late at night, but this London moved with the decorum and caution of an undertaker. There was a silence, and yet there was no silence. There was a low drone, perhaps a humming contributed inevitably by closely-gathered thousands, and yet on second thoughts it was to me silence. I had perched my ears for the note of London, the sound made simply by the existence of five million people in one place. I had imagined something deep, vastly deep, a bass from a mythical organ, but found as far as I was concerned, only a silence.

New York in numbers is a mighty city, and all day and all night it cries its loud, fierce, aspiring cry, a noise of men beating upon barrels, a noise of men beating upon tin, a terrific racket that assails the abject skies. No one of us seemed to question this row as a certain consequence of three or four million people living together and scuffling for coin, with more agility, perhaps, but otherwise in the usual way. However, after this easy silence of London, which in numbers is a mightier city, I began to feel that there was a se-

duction in this idea of necessity. Our noise in New York
was not a consequence of our rapidity at all. It was a consequence of our bad pavements.

Any brigade of artillery in Europe that would love to
assemble its batteries, and then go on a gallop over the
land, thundering and thundering, would give up the idea
of thunder at once if it could hear Tim Mulligan drive a
beer wagon along one of the side streets of cobbled New
York.

CHAPTER III

FINALLY a great thing came to pass. The cab horse, pro-
ceeding at a sharp trot, found himself suddenly at the top
of an incline, where through the rain the pavement shone
like an expanse of ice. It looked to me as if there was going
to be a tumble. In an accident of such a kind a hansom
becomes really a cannon in which a man finds that he has
paid shillings for the privilege of serving as a projectile. I
was making a rapid calculation of the arc that I would describe in my flight, when the horse met his crisis with a
masterly device that I could not have imagined. He tranquilly braced his four feet like a bundle of stakes, and then,
with a gentle gaiety of demeanor, he slid swiftly and grace-
fully to the bottom of the hill as if he had been a toboggan.
When the incline ended he caught his gait again with great
dexterity, and went pattering off through another tunnel.

I at once looked upon myself as being singularly blessed
by this sight. This horse had evidently originated this sys-
tem of skating as a diversion, or, more probably, as a pre-

caution against the slippery pavement; and he was, of course, the inventor and sole proprietor—two terms that are not always in conjunction. It surely was not to be supposed that there could be two skaters like him in the world. He deserved to be known and publicly praised for this accomplishment. It was worthy of many records and exhibitions. But when the cab arrived at a place where some dipping streets met, and the flaming front of a music-hall temporarily widened my cylinder, behold there were many cabs, and as the moment of necessity came the horses were all skaters. They were gliding in all directions. It might have been a rink. A great omnibus was hailed by a hand under an umbrella on the side walk, and the dignified horses bidden to halt from their trot did not waste time in wild and unseemly spasms. They, too, braced their legs and slid gravely to the end of their momentum.

It was not the feat, but it was the word which had at this time the power to conjure memories of skating parties on moonlit lakes, with laughter ringing over the ice, and a great red bonfire on the shore among the hemlocks.

CHAPTER IV

A TERRIBLE thing in nature is the fall of a horse in his harness. It is a tragedy. Despite their skill in skating there was that about the pavement on the rainy evening which filled me with expectations of horses going headlong. Finally it happened just in front. There was a shout and a tangle in the darkness, and presently a prostrate cab horse came within my cylinder. The accident having been a complete success and altogether concluded, a voice from the side walk said, "*Look* out, now! *Be* more careful, can't you?"

I remember a constituent of a Congressman at Washington who had tried in vain to bore this Congressman with a wild project of some kind. The Congressman eluded him with skill, and his rage and despair ultimately culminated in the supreme grievance that he could not even get near enough to the Congressman to tell him to go to Hades.

This cabman should have felt the same desire to strangle this man who spoke from the sidewalk. He was plainly impotent; he was deprived of the power of looking out. There was nothing now for which to look out. The man on the sidewalk had dragged a corpse from a pond and said to it, "*Be* more careful, can't you, or you'll drown?" My cabman pulled up and addressed a few words of reproach to the other. Three or four figures loomed into my cylinder, and as they appeared spoke to the author or the victim of the calamity in varied terms of displeasure. Each of these reproaches was couched in terms that defined the situation as impending. No blind man could have conceived that the precipitate phrase of the incident was absolutely closed.

"*Look* out now, cawn't you?" And there was nothing in his mind which approached these sentiments near enough to tell them to go to Hades.

However, it needed only an ear to know presently that these expressions were formulæ. It was merely the obligatory dance which the Indians had to perform before they went to war. These men had come to help, but as a regular and traditional preliminary they had first to display to this cabman their idea of his ignominy.

The different thing in the affair was the silence of the victim. He retorted never a word. This, too, to me seemed to be an obedience to a recognized form. He was the visible criminal, if there was a criminal, and there was born of it a privilege for them.

They unfastened the proper straps and hauled back the cab. They fetched a mat from some obscure place of succor, and pushed it carefully under the prostrate thing. From this panting, quivering mass they suddenly and emphatically reconstructed a horse. As each man turned to go his way he delivered some superior caution to the cabman while the latter buckled his harness.

CHAPTER V

THERE was to be noticed in this band of rescuers a young man in evening clothes and top-hat. Now, in America a young man in evening clothes and a top-hat may be a terrible object. He is not likely to do violence, but he is likely to do impassivity and indifference to the point where they become worse than violence. There are certain of the more idle phases of civilization to which America has not yet awakened—and it is a matter of no moment if she remains unaware. This matter of hats is one of them. I recall a legend recited to me by an esteemed friend, ex-Sheriff of Tin Can, Nevada. Jim Cortright, one of the best gunfighters in town, went on a journey to Chicago, and while there he procured a top-hat. He was quite sure how Tin Can would accept this innovation, but he relied on the celerity with which he could get a six-shooter in action. One

Sunday Jim examined his guns with his usual care, placed the top-hat on the back of his head, and sauntered coolly out into the streets of Tin Can.

Now, while Jim was in Chicago some progressive citizen had decided that Tin Can needed a bowling alley. The carpenters went to work the next morning, and an order for the balls and pins was telegraphed to Denver. In three days the whole population was concentrated at the new alley betting their outfits and their lives.

It has since been accounted very unfortunate that Jim Cortright had not learned of bowling alleys at his mother's knee or even later in the mines. This portion of his mind was singularly belated. He might have been an Apache for all he knew of bowling alleys.

In his careless stroll through the town, his hands not far from his belt and his eyes going sideways in order to see who would shoot first at the hat, he came upon this long, low shanty where Tin Can was betting itself hoarse over a game between a team from the ranks of Excelsior Hose Company No. 1 and a team composed from the *habitues* of the "Red Light" saloon.

Jim, in blank ignorance of bowling phenomena, wandered casually through a little door into what must always be termed the wrong end of a bowling alley. Of course, he saw that the supreme moment had come. They were not only shooting at the hat and at him, but the low-down cusses were using the most extraordinary and hellish ammunition. Still, perfectly undaunted, however, Jim retorted with his two Colts, and killed three of the best bowlers in Tin Can.

The ex-Sheriff vouched for this story. He himself had

gone headlong through the door at the firing of the first shot with that simple courtesy which leads Western men to donate the fighters plenty of room. He said that afterwards the hat was the cause of a number of other fights, and that finally a delegation of prominent citizens was obliged to wait upon Cortright and ask him if he wouldn't take that thing away somewhere and bury it. Jim pointed out to them that it was his hat, and that he would regard it as a cowardly concession if he submitted to their dictation in the matter of his headgear. He added that he purposed to continue to wear his top-hat on every occasion when he happened to feel that the wearing of a top-hat was a joy and a solace to him.

The delegation sadly retired, and announced to the town that Jim Cortright had openly defied them, and had declared his purpose of forcing his top-hot on the pained attention of Tin Can whenever he chose. Jim Cortright's plug hat became a phrase with considerable meaning to it.

However, the whole affair ended in a great passionate outburst of popular revolution. Spike Foster was a friend of Cortright, and one day, when the latter was indisposed, Spike came to him and borrowed the hat. He had been drinking heavily at the "Red Light," and was in a supremely reckless mood. With the terrible gear hanging jauntily over his eye and his two guns drawn, he walked straight out into the middle of the square in front of the Palace Hotel, and drew the attention of all Tin Can by a blood-curdling imitation of the yowl of a mountain lion.

This was when the long suffering populace arose as one man. The top-hat had been flaunted once too often. When

Spike Foster's friends came to carry him away they found
nearly a hundred and fifty men shooting busily at a mark
—and the mark was the hat.

My informant told me that he believed he owed his popu-
larity in Tin Can, and subsequently his election to the dis-
tinguished office of Sheriff, to the active and prominent part
he had taken in the proceedings.

The enmity to the top-hat expressed by the convincing
anecdote exists in the American West at present, I think, in
the perfection of its strength; but disapproval is not now
displayed by volleys from the citizens, save in the most ag-
gravating cases.   It is at present usually a matter of mere
jibe and general contempt.   The East, however, despite a
great deal of kicking and gouging, is having the top-hat
stuffed slowly and carefully down its throat, and there now
exist many young men who consider that they could not
successfully conduct their lives without this furniture.

To speak generally, I should say that the headgear then
supplies them with a kind of ferocity of indifference.   There
is fire, sword, and pestilence in the way they heed only themselves.   Philosophy should always know that indifference is
a militant thing.   It batters down the walls of cities, and
murders the women and children amid flames and the pur-
loining of altar vessels.   When it goes away it leaves smoking ruins, where lie citizens bayoneted through the throat.
It is not a children's pastime like mere highway robbery.

Consequently in America we may be much afraid of these
young men.   We dive down alleys so that we may not kow-
tow.   It is a fearsome thing.

Taught thus a deep fear of the top-hat in its effect upon

youth, I was not prepared for the move of this particular young man when the cab-horse fell. In fact, I grovelled in my corner that I might not see the cruel stateliness of his passing. But in the meantime he had crossed the street, and contributed the strength of his back and some advice as well as the formal address, to the cabman on the importance of looking out immediately.

I felt that I was making a notable collection. I had a new kind of porter, a cylinder of vision, horses that could skate, and now I added a young man in a top-hat who would tacitly admit that the beings around him were alive. He was not walking a churchyard filled with inferior headstones. He was walking the world, where there were people, many people.

But later I took him out of the collection. I thought he had rebelled against the manner of a class, but I soon discovered that the top-hat was not the property of a class. It was the property of rogues, clerks, theatrical agents, damned seducers, poor men, nobles, and others. In fact, it was the universal rigging. It was the only hat; all other forms might as well be named ham, or chops, or oysters. I retracted my admiration of the young man because he may have been merely a rogue.

CHAPTER VI

THERE was a window whereat an enterprising man by dodging two placards and a calendar was entitled to view a young woman. She was dejectedly writing in a large book. She was ultimately induced to open the window a trifle

"What nyme, please?" she said wearily. I was surprised
to hear this language from her. I had expected to be addressed on a submarine topic. I have seen shell fishes sadly
writing in large books at the bottom of a gloomy acquarium
who could not ask me what was my "nyme."

At the end of the hall there was a grim portal marked
"Lift." I pressed an electric button and heard an answering
tinkle in the heavens. There was an upholstered settle near
at hand, and I discovered the reason. A deer-stalking peace
drooped upon everything, and in it a man could invoke the
passing of a lazy pageant of twenty years of his life.

The dignity of a coffin being lowered into a grave surrounded the ultimate appearance of the lift. The expert
we in America call the elevator-boy stepped from the car,
took three paces forward, faced to attention and saluted.
This elevator boy could not have been less than sixty years
of age; a great white beard streamed towards his belt. I
saw that the lift had been longer on its voyage than I had
suspected.

Later in our upward progress a natural event would have
been an establishment of social relations. Two enemies im-
prisoned together during the still hours of a balloon journey
would, I believe, suffer a mental amalgamation. The over-
hang of a common fate, a great principal fact, can make
an equality and a truce between any pair. Yet, when I
disembarked, a final survey of the grey beard made me recall that I had failed even to ask the boy whether he had
not taken probably three trips on this lift.

My windows overlooked simply a great sea of night, in
which were swimming little gas fishes.

CHAPTER VII

I HAVE of late been led to reflect wistfully that many of the illustrators are very clever. In an impatience, which was donated by a certain economy of apparel, I went to a window to look upon day-lit London. There were the 'buses parading the streets with the miens of elephants. There were the police looking precisely as I had been informed by the prints. There were the sandwich-men. There was almost everything.

But the artists had not told me the sound of London. Now, in New York the artists are able to portray sound, because in New York a dray is not a dray at all; it is a great potent noise hauled by two or more horses. When a magazine containing an illustration of a New York street is sent to me, I always know it beforehand. I can hear it coming through the mails. As I have said previously, this which I must call sound of London was to me only a silence.

Later, in front of the hotel a cabman that I hailed said to me—"Are you gowing far, sir? I've got a byby here, and want to giv'er a bit of a blough." This impressed me as being probably a quotation from an early Egyptian poet, but I learned soon enough that the word "byby" was the name of some kind or condition of horse. The cabman's next remark was addressed to a boy who took a perilous dive between the byby's nose and a cab in front. "That's roight. Put your head in there and get it jammed—a whackin good place for it, I should think." Although the tone was low and circumspect, I have never heard a better off-handed declamation. Every word was cut clear of disreputable alliances with its neighbors. The whole thing was as clean as a row of pewter mugs. The influence of indignation upon the voice caused me to reflect that we might devise a mechanical means of inflaming some in that constellation of mummers which is the heritage of the Anglo-Saxon race.

Then I saw the drilling of vehicles by two policemen. There were four torrents converging at a point, and when four torrents converge at one point engineering experts buy tickets for another place.

But here, again, it was drill, plain, simple drill. I must not falter in saying that I think the management of the traffic—as the phrase goes—to be distinctly illuminating and wonderful. The police were not ruffled and exasperated. They were as peaceful as two cows in a pasture.

I can remember once remarking that mankind, with all its boasted modern progress, had not yet been able to invent a turnstile that will commute in fractions. I have now learned that 756 rights-of-way cannot operate simultaneously at one point. Right-of-way, like fighting women, requires space. Even two rights-of-way can make a scene which is only suited to the tastes of an ancient public.

This truth was very evidently reocgnized. There was only one right-of-way at a time. The police did not look behind them to see if their orders were to be obeyed; they knew they were to be obeyed. These four torrents were drilling like four battalions. The two blue-cloth men maneuvered them in solemn, abiding peace, the silence of London.

I thought at first that it was the intellect of the individual, but I looked at one constable closely and his face was as afire with intelligence as a flannel pin-cushion. It was not the police, and it was not the crowd. It was the police and the crowd. Again, it was drill.

CHAPTER VIII

I HAVE never been in the habit of reading signs. I don't like to read signs. I have never met a man that liked to read signs. I once invented a creature who could play the piano with a hammer, and I mentioned him to a professor in Harvard University whose peculiarity was Sanscrit. He had the same interest in my invention that I have in a certain kind of mustard. And yet this mustard has become a part of me. Or, I have become a part of this mustard. Further, I know more of an ink, a brand of hams, a kind of cigarette, and a novelist than any man living. I went by train to see a friend in the country, and after passing through a patent mucilage, some more hams, a South African Investment Company, a Parisian millinery firm, and a comic journal, I alighted at a new and original kind of corset. On my return journey the road almost continuously ran through soap.

I have accumulated superior information concerning these things, because I am at their mercy. If I want to know where I am I must find the definitive sign. This accounts for my glib use of the word mucilage, as well as the titles of other staples.

I suppose even the Briton in mixing his life must sometimes consult the labels on 'buses and streets and stations, even as the chemist consults the labels on his bottles and boxes. A brave man would possibly affirm that this was suggested by the existence of the labels.

The reason that I did not learn more about hams and mucilage in New York seems to me to be partly due to the fact that the British advertiser is allowed to exercise an unbridled strategy in his attack with his new corset or whatever upon the defensive public. He knows that the vulnerable point is the informatory sign which the citizen must, of course, use for his guidance, and then, with horse, foot, guns, corsets, hams, mucilage, investment companies, and all, he hurls himself at the point.

Meanwhile I have discovered a way to make the Sanscrit scholar heed my creature who plays the piano with a hammer.

THE SCOTCH EXPRESS

THE SCOTCH EXPRESS

THE entrance to Euston Station is of itself sufficiently imposing. It is a high portico of brown stone, old and grim, in form a casual imitation, no doubt, of the front of the temple of Nike Apteros, with a recollection of the Egyptians proclaimed at the flanks. The frieze, where of old would prance an exuberant processional of gods, is, in this case, bare of decoration, but upon the epistyle is written in simple, stern letters the word "EUSTON." The legend reared high by the gloomy Pelagic columns stares down a wide avenue. In short, this entrance to a railway station does not in any way resemble the entrance to a railway station. It is more the front of some venerable bank. But it has another dignity, which is not born of form. To a great degree, it is to the English and to those who are in England the gate to Scotland.

The little hansoms are continually speeding through the gate, dashing between the legs of the solemn temple; the four-wheelers, their tops crowded with luggage, roll in and out constantly, and the footways beat under the trampling of the people. Of course, there are the suburbs and a hundred towns along the line, and Liverpool, the beginning of an important sea-path to America, and the great manufacturing cities of the North; but if one stands at this gate in August particularly, one must note the number of men with gun-cases, the number of women who surely have Tam-o'-Shanters and plaids concealed within their luggage, ready for the moors. There is, during the latter part of that month, a wholesale flight from London to Scotland which recalls the July throngs leaving New York for the shore or the mountains.

The hansoms, after passing through this impressive portal of the station, bowl smoothly across a courtyard which is in the center of the terminal hotel, an institution dear to most railways in Europe. The traveler lands amid a swarm of porters, and then proceeds cheerfully to take the customary trouble for his luggage. America provides a contrivance in a thousand situations where Europe provides a man or perhaps a number of men, and the work of our brass check is here done by porters, directed by the traveler himself. The men lack the memory of the check; the check never forgets its identity. Moreover, the European railways generously furnish the porters at the expense of the traveler. Nevertheless, if these men have not the invincible business precision of the check, and if they have to be tipped, it can be asserted for those who care that in Europe one-half of the populace waits on the other half most diligently and well.

Against the masonry of a platform, under the vaulted arch of the train-house, lay a long string of coaches. They were painted white on the bulging part, which led halfway down from the top, and the bodies were a deep bottle-green. There was a group of porters placing luggage in the van, and a great many others were busy with the affairs of passengers, tossing smaller bits of luggage into the racks over the seats,

The train swung impressively around the signal-house, and headed up a brick-walled cut. In starting this heavy string of coaches, the engine breathed explosively. It gasped, and heaved, and bellowed; once, for a moment, the wheels spun on the rails, and a convulsive tremor shook the great steel frame.

The train itself, however, moved through this deep cut in the body of London with coolness and precision, and the employees of the railway, knowing the train's mission, tacitly presented arms at its passing. To the travelers in the carriages, the suburbs of London must have been one long monotony of carefully made walls of stone or brick. But after the hill was climbed, the train fled through pictures of red habitations of men on a green earth.

But the noise in the cab did not greatly change its measure. Even though the speed was now high, the tremendous thumping to be heard in the cab was as alive with strained effort and as slow in beat as the breathing of a half-drowned man. At the side of the track, for instance, the sound doubtless would strike the ear in the familiar succession of incredibly rapid puffs; but in the cab itself, this land-racer breathes very like its friend, the marine engine. Everybody who has spent time on shipboard has forever in his head a reminiscence of the steady and methodical pounding of the engines, and perhaps it is curious that this relative which can whirl over the land at such a pace, breathes in the leisurely tones that a man heeds when he lies awake at night in his berth.

There had been no fog in London, but here on the edge of the city a heavy wind was blowing, and the driver leaned aside and yelled that it was a very bad day for traveling on an engine. The engine-cabs of England, as of all Europe, are seldom made for the comfort of the men. One finds very often this apparent disregard for the man who does the work—this indifference to the man who occupies a position which for the exercise of temperance, of courage, of honesty, has no equal at the altitude of prime ministers. The American engineer is the gilded occupant of a salon in comparison with his brother in Europe. The man who was guiding this five-hundred-ton bolt, aimed by the officials of the railway at Scotland, could not have been as comfortable as a shrill gibbering boatman of the Orient. The narrow and bare bench at his side of the cab was not directly intended for his use, because it was so low that he would be prevented by it from looking out of the ship's port-hole which served him as a window. The fireman, on his side, had other difficulties. His legs would have had to straggle over some pipes at the only spot where there was a prospect, and the builders had also strategically placed a large steel bolt. Of course it is plain that the companies consistently believe that the men will do their work better if they are kept standing. The roof of the cab was not altogether a roof. It was merely a projection of two feet of metal from the bulkhead which formed the front of the cab. There were practically no sides to it, and the large cinders from the soft coal whirled around in sheets. From time to time the driver took a handkerchief from his pocket and wiped his blinking eyes.

London was now well to the rear. The vermilion engine had been for some time flying like the wind. This train averages, between London and Carlisle forty-nine and nine-

a bridge or a tunnel. The platforms of even the remote country stations were all of ponderous masonry in contrast to our constructions of planking. There was always to be seen, as we thundered toward a station of this kind, a number of porters in uniform, who requested the retreat of any one who had not the wit to give us plenty of room. And then, as the shrill warning of the whistle pierced even the uproar that was about us, came the wild joy of the rush past a station. It was something in the nature of a triumphal procession conducted at thrilling speed. Perhaps there was a curve of infinite grace, a sudden hollow explosive effect made by the passing of a signal-box that was close to the track, and then the deadly lunge to shave the edge of a long platform. There were always a number of people standing afar, with their eyes riveted upon this projectile, and to be on the engine was to feel their interest and admiration in the terror and grandeur of this sweep. A boy allowed to ride with the driver of the band-wagon as a circus parade winds through one of our village streets could not exceed for egotism the temper of a new man in the cab of a train like this one. This valkyric journey on the back of the vermilion engine, with the shouting of the wind, the deep, mighty panting of the steed, the gray blur at the track-side, the flowing quicksilver ribbon of the other rails, the sudden clash as a switch intersects, all the din and fury of this ride, was of a splendor that caused one to look abroad at the quiet, green landscape and believe that it was of a phlegm quiet beyond patience. It should have been dark, rain-shot, and windy; thunder should have rolled across its sky.

It seemed, somehow, that if the driver should for a mo-

ment take his hands from his engine, it might swerve from
the track as a horse from the road. Once, indeed, as he stood
wiping his fingers on a bit of waste, there must have been
something ludicrous in the way the solitary passenger regarded him. Without those finely firm hands on the bridle,
the engine might rear and bolt for the pleasant farms lying
in the sunshine at either side.

This driver was worth contemplation. He was simply a
quiet, middle-aged man, bearded, and with the little wrinkles
of habitual geniality and kindliness spreading from the eyes
toward the temple, who stood at his post always gazing out,
through his round window, while, from time to time, his
hands went from here to there over his levers. He seldom
changed either attitude or expression. There surely is no
engine-driver who does not feel the beauty of the business,
but the emotion lies deep, and mainly inarticulate, as it does
in the mind of a man who has experienced a good and beautiful wife for many years. This driver's face displayed nothing but the cool sanity of a man whose thought was buried
intelligently in his business. If there was any fierce drama
in it, there was no sign upon him. He was so lost in dreams
of speed and signals and steam, that one speculated if the
wonder of his tempestuous charge and its career over England touched him, this impassive rider of a fiery thing.

It should be a well-known fact that, all over the world, the
engine-driver is the finest type of man that is grown. He is
the pick of the earth. He is altogether more worthy than
the soldier, and better than the men who move on the sea in
ships. He is not paid too much; nor do his glories weight
his brow; but for outright performance, carried on constantly,

coolly, and without elation, by a temperate, honest, clear-minded man, he is the further point. And so the lone human at his station in a cab, guarding money, lives, and the honor of the road, is a beautiful sight. The whole thing is æsthetic. The fireman presents the same charm, but in a less degree, in that he is bound to appear as an apprentice to the finished manhood of the driver. In his eyes, turned always in question and confidence toward his superior, one finds this quality; but his aspirations are so direct that one sees the same type in evolution.

There may be a popular idea that the fireman's principal function is to hang his head out of the cab and sight interesting objects in the landscape. As a matter of fact, he is always at work. The dragon is insatiate. The fireman is continually swinging open the furnace-door, whereat a red shine flows out upon the floor of the cab, and shoveling in immense mouthfuls of coal to a fire that is almost diabolic in its madness. The feeding, feeding, feeding goes on until it appears as if it is the muscles of the fireman's arms that are speeding the long train. An engine running over sixty-five miles an hour, with 500 tons to drag, has an appetite in proportion to this task.

View of the clear-shining English scenery is often interrupted between London and Crew by long and short tunnels. the first one was disconcerting. Suddenly one knew that the train was shooting toward a black mouth in the hills. It swiftly yawned wider, and then in a moment the engine dived into a place inhabited by every demon of wind and noise. The speed had not been checked, and the uproar was so great that in effect one was simply standing at the center of a vast, black-walled sphere. The tubular construction which one's reason proclaimed had no meaning at all. It was a black sphere, alive with shrieks. But then on the surface of it there was to be seen a little needle-point of light, and this widened to a detail of unreal landscape. It was the world; the train was going to escape from this cauldron, this abyss of howling darkness. If a man looks through the brilliant water of a tropical pool, he can sometimes see coloring the marvels at the bottom the blue that was on the sky and the green that was on the foliage of this detail. And the picture shimmered in the heat-rays of a new and remarkable sun. It was when the train bolted out into the open air that one knew that it was his own earth.

Once train met train in a tunnel. Upon the painting in the perfectly circular frame formed by the mouth there appeared a black square with sparks bursting from it. This square expanded until it hid everything, and a moment later came the crash of the passing. It was enough to make a man lose his sense of balance. It was a momentary inferno when the fireman opened the furnace door and was bathed in blood-red light as he fed the fires.

The effect of a tunnel varied when there was a curve in it. One was merely whirling then heels over head, apparently in the dark, echoing bowels of the earth. There was no needle-point of light to which one's eyes clung as to a star.

From London to Crew, the stern arm of the semaphore never made the train pause even for an instant. There was always a clear track. It was great to see, far in the distance, a goods train whooping smokily for the north of England on one of the four tracks. The overtaking of such a train was a thing of magnificent nothing for the long-strided engine, and as the flying express passed its weaker brother, one heard one or two feeble and immature puffs from the other engine, saw the fireman wave his hand to his luckier fellow, saw a string of foolish, clanking flat-cars, their freights covered with tarpaulins, and then the train was lost to the rear.

The driver twisted his wheel and worked some levers, and the rhythmical chunking of the engine gradually ceased. Gliding at a speed that was still high, the train curved to the left, and swung down a sharp incline, to move with an imperial dignity through the railway yard at Rugby. There was a maze of switches, innumerable engines noisily pushing cars here and there, crowds of workmen who turned to look, a sinuous curve around the long train-shed, whose high wall resounded with the rumble of the passing express; and then, almost immediately, it seemed, came the open country again. Rugby had been a dream which one could properly doubt. At last the relaxed engine, with the same majesty of ease, swung into the high-roofed station at Crewe, and stopped on a platform lined with porters and citizens. There was instant bustle, and in the interest of the moment no one seemed particularly to notice the tired vermilion engine being led away.

There is a five-minute stop at Crewe. A tandem of engines slip up, and buckled fast to the train for the journey to Carlisle. In the meantime, all the regulation items of peace and comfort had happened on the train itself. The dining-car was in the center of the train. It was divided into two parts, the one being a dining-room for first-class passengers, and the other a dining-room for the third-class passengers. They were separated by the kitchens and the larder. The engine, with all its rioting and roaring, had dragged to Crewe a car in which numbers of passengers were lunching in a tranquility that was almost domestic, on an average menu of a chop and potatoes, a salad, cheese, and a bottle of beer. Betimes they watched through the windows the great chimney-marked towns of northern England. They were waited upon by a young man of London, who was supported by a lad who resembled an American bell-boy. The rather elaborate menu and service of the Pullman dining-car is not known in England or on the Continent. Warmed roast beef is the exact symbol of a European dinner, when one is traveling on a railway.

This express is named, both by the public and the company, the "Corridor Train," because a coach with a corridor is an unusual thing in England, and so the title has a distinctive meaning. Of course, in America, where there is no car which has not what we call an aisle, it would define nothing. The corridors are all at one side of the car. Doors open thence to little compartments made to seat four, or perhaps six, persons. The first-class carriages are very comfortable indeed, being heavily upholstered in dark, hard-wearing stuffs, with a bulging rest for the head. The third-class accommodations on this train are almost as comfortable as the first-class, and attract a kind of people that are not usually seen traveling third-class in Europe. Many people sacrifice their habit, in the matter of this train, to the fine conditions of the lower fare.

One of the feats of the train is an electric button in each compartment. Commonly an electric button is placed high on the side of the carriage as an alarm signal, and it is unlawful to push it unless one is in serious need of assistance from the guard. But these bells also rang in the dining-car, and were supposed to open negotiations for tea or whatever. A new function has been projected on an ancient custom. No genius has yet appeared to separate these two meanings. Each bell rings an alarm and a bid for tea or whatever. It is perfect in theory then that, if one rings for tea, the guard comes to interrupt the murder, and that if one is being murdered, the attendant appears with tea. At any rate, the guard was forever being called from his reports and his comfortable seat in the forward end of the luggage-van by thrilling alarms. He often prowled the length of the train with hardihood and determination, merely to meet a request for a sandwich.

The train entered Carlisle at the beginning of twilight. This is the border town, and an engine of the Caledonian Railway, manned by two men of broad speech, came to take the place of the tandem. The engine of these men of the North was much smaller than the others, but her cab was much larger, and would be a fair shelter on a stormy night. They had also built seats with hooks by which they hang them to the rail, and thus are still enabled to see through the round windows without dislocating their necks. All the human parts of the cab were covered with oilcloth. The wind that swirled from the dim twilight horizon made the warm glow from the furnace to be a grateful thing.

As the train shot out of Carlisle, a glance backward could learn of the faint, yellow blocks of light from the carriages marked on the dimmed ground. The signals were now lamps, and shone palely against the sky. The express was entering night as if night were Scotland.

There was a long toil to the summit of the hills, and then began the booming ride down the slope. There were many curves. Sometimes could be seen two or three signal lights at one time, twisting off in some new direction. Minus the lights and some yards of glistening rails, Scotland was only a blend of black and weird shapes. Forests which one could hardly imagine as weltering in the dewy placidity of evening sank to the rear as if the gods had bade them. The dark loom of a house quickly dissolved before the eyes. A station with its lamps became a broad yellow band that, to a deficient sense, was only a few yards in length. Below, in a deep valley, a silver glare on the waters of a river made equal time with the train. Signals appeared, grew, and vanished. In the wind and the mystery of the night, it was like sailing in an enchanted gloom. The vague profiles of hills ran like snakes across the somber sky. A strange shape boldly and formidably confronted the train, and then melted to a long dash of track as clean as sword-blades.

The vicinity of Glasgow is unmistakable. The flames of pauseless industries are here and there marked on the distance. Vast factories stand close to the track, and reaching chimneys emit roseate flames. At last one may see upon a wall the strong reflection from furnaces, and against it the impish and inky figures of workingmen. A long, prison-like row of tenements, not at all resembling London, but in one way resembling New York, appeared to the left, and then sank out of sight like a phantom.

At last the driver stopped the brave effort of his engine.

The 400 miles were come to the edge. The average speed of forty-nine and one-third miles each hour had been made, and it remained only to glide with the hauteur of a great express through the yard and into the station at Glasgow.

A wide and splendid collection of signal lamps flowed toward the engine. With delicacy and care the train clanked over some switches, passes the signals, and then there shone a great blaze of arc-lamps, defining the wide sweep of the station roof. Smoothly, proudly, with all that vast dignity which had surrounded its exit from London, the express moved along its platform. It was the entrance into a gorgeous drawing-room of a man that was sure of everything.

The porters and the people crowded forward. In their minds there may have floated dim images of the traditional music-halls, the bobbies, the 'buses, the 'Arrys and 'Arriets, the swells of London.

THE END

THE MODERN LIBRARY
OF THE WORLD'S BEST BOOKS
Hand Bound in Limp Binding, Stained Tops, Gold Decorations, only 95c. per copy
Postage 5c. per copy extra

FIVE years ago, the Modern Library of the World's Best Books made is appearance with twelve titles. It was immediately recognized, to quote the New York Times, "as filling a need that is not quite covered by any other publication in the field just now." The Dial hastened to say "The moderns put their best foot forward in the Modern Library. There is scarcely a title that fails to awaken interest and the series is doubly welcome at this time." A week or so after the publication of the first titles, The Independent wrote: "The Modern Library is another step in the very right direction of putting good books into inexpensive form," and the clever Editor of the Chicago Daily News, in a long review, concluded: "The Modern Library astonishes the cynical with the excellence of its choice of titles. You could stand before a stack of these books, shut your eyes and pick out the right one every time." Despite this enthusiasm, in publishing circles it was considered impossible to continue the sale of these attractive Hand Bound Limp books, printed in large clear type on good paper, at any price under the usual and prevailing price charged for the more cheaply made current fiction, which is now about Two Dollars a volume. But the large number of intelligent book buyers, a much larger group than is generally supposed, has not only made possible the continuation of this fine series at the low price of Ninety-five Cents a volume, but has enabled us progressively to make it a better and more comprehensive collection. There are now eighty-nine titles in the series and from eight to fifteen new ones are being added each Spring and Fall. And in mechanical excellence, too, the books have been constantly improved.

Complete List of Titles

For convenience in ordering please use number at right of title

A MODERN BOOK OF CRITICISMS (81) Edited with an
Introduction by LUDWIG LEWISOHN
ANDERSON, SHERWOOD (1876-)
Winesburg, Ohio, (104)
ANDREYEV, LEONID (1871-)
The Seven That Were Hanged and The Red Laugh **(45)**
Introduction by THOMAS SELTZER
ATHERTON, GERTRUDE (1859-)
Rezanov (71) Introduction by WILLIAM MARION REEDY
BALZAC, HONORE DE (1799-1850)
Short Stories (40)
BAUDELAIRE, PIERRE CHARLES (1821-1867)
His Prose and Poetry (70)
BEARDSLEY, THE ART OF AUBREY (1872-1898)
64 Black and White Reproductions (42) Introduction by
ARTHUR SYMONS
BEERBOHM, MAX (1872-)
Zuleika Dobson (50) Introduction by FRANCIS HACKETT
BEST GHOST STORIES (73)
Introduction by ARTHUR B. REEVE
BEST HUMOROUS AMERICAN SHORT STORIES (87)
Edited with an Introduction by ALEXANDER JESSUP
BEST RUSSIAN SHORT STORIES (18)
Edited with an Introduction by THOMAS SELTZER
BLAKE, WILLIAM (1757-1827)
Poems (91) Edited with notes by WILLIAM BUTLER YEATS
BUTLER, SAMUEL (1835-1902)
The Way of All Flesh (13)
CARPENTER, EDWARD (1844-)
Love's Coming of Age (51)
CHEKHOV, ANTON (1860-1904)
Rothschild's Fiddle and Thirteen Other Stories (31)
CHESTERTON, G. K. (1874-)
The Man Who Was Thursday (35)
CONTEMPORARY SCIENCE (99)
Edited with an Introduction by Dr. BENJ. HARROW
CRANE, STEPHEN (1870-)
Men, Women and Boats (102) Introduction by VINCENT
STARRETT
D'ANNUNZIO, GABRIELE (1864-)
The Flame of Life (65)
The Triumph of Death (112) Introduction by BURTON
RASCOE
DAUDET, ALPHONSE (1840-1897)
Sapho (85) In same volume Prevost's **"Manon Lescaut"**

Modern Library of the World's Best Books

Modern Library of the World's Best Books

tenth miles an hour. It is a distance of 299 miles. There is one stop. It occurs at Crewe, and endures five minutes. In consequence, the block signals flashed by seemingly at the end of the moment in which they were sighted.

There can be no question of the statement that the road-beds of English railways are at present immeasurably superior to the American road-beds. Of course there is a clear reason. It is known to every traveler that peoples of the Continent of Europe have no right at all to own railways. Those lines of travel are too childish and trivial for expression. A correct fate would deprive the Continent of its railways, and give them to somebody who knew about them. The continental idea of a railway is to surround a mass of machinery with forty rings of ultra-military law, and then they believe they have one complete. The Americans and the English are the railway peoples. That our road-beds are poorer than the English road-beds is because of the fact that we were suddenly obliged to build thousands upon thousands of miles of railway, and the English were obliged to build slowly tens upon tens of miles. A road-bed from New York to San Francisco, with stations, bridges, and crossings of the kind that the London and Northwestern owns from London to Glasgow, would cost a sum large enough to support the German army for a term of years. The whole way is constructed with the care that inspired the creators of some of our now obsolete forts along the Atlantic coast. An American engineer, with his knowledge of the difficulties he had to encounter—the wide rivers with variable banks, the mountain chains, perhaps the long spaces of absolute desert; in fact, all the perplexities of a vast and somewhat new country—would not dare spend a respectable portion of his allowance on seventy feet of granite wall over a gully, when he knew he could make an embankment with little cost by heaving up the dirt and stones from here and there. But the English road is all made in the pattern by which the Romans built their highways. After England is dead, savants will find narrow streaks of masonry leading from ruin to ruin. Of course this does not always seem convincingly admirable. It sometimes resembles energy poured into a rat-hole. There is a vale between expediency and the convenience of posterity, a mid-ground which enables men surely to benefit the hereafter people by valiantly advancing the present; and the point is that, if some laborers live in unhealthy tenements in Cornwall, one is likely to view with incomplete satisfaction the record of long and patient labor and thought displayed by an eight-foot drain for a non-existent, impossible rivulet in the North. This sentence does not sound strictly fair, but the meaning one wishes to convey is that if an English company spies in its dream the ghost of an ancient valley that later becomes a hill, it would construct for it a magnificent steel trestle, and consider that a duty had been performed in proper accordance with the company's conscience. But after all is said of it, the accidents and the miles of railway operated in England are not in proportion to the accidents and the miles of railway operated in the United States. The reason can be divided into three parts—older conditions, superior caution, the road-bed. And of these, the greatest is older conditions.

In this flight toward Scotland one seldom encountered a grade crossing. In nine cases of of ten there was either